CURSE OF THE SHADOWS

The Shadow Hunt series

Book 2

IAN FORTEY

AND

RON RIPLEY

EDITED BY ANNE LAO
AND DAWN KLEMISH

ISBN: 979-8-89476-282-1
Copyright © 2025 by ScareStreet.com

ENTER THE REALM OF TERROR...

We'd like to take a moment to thank you for your support and invite you to join our VIP newsletter.

Dive deeper into the darkness with exclusive offers, early access to new releases, and bone-chilling deals when you sign up at www.ScareStreet.com.

Let the nightmares begin...

See you in the shadows,
Scare Street

PROLOGUE

The tops of the corn stalks were well past seven feet tall. When the breeze blew strongly enough, the wide, rough leaves rustled together, and the sound was like a thousand harried whispers. The cornfield was telling secrets, Paul's grandmother used to say.

In the height of summer, those leaves scraped and grated even more loudly. The difference was hard to notice with just one plant. But get a few hundred thousand together, all five inches apart, and the whispers were like a symphony of secrets. At night, it could become terrifying.

When Paul was a child, he couldn't sleep on stormy nights because of the cornfield. Once it started raining, it was not a big deal. But in those moments leading up to it, which could sometimes take an hour or more, it was like enduring a waking nightmare in the darkness of his room on the third floor of the house all by himself.

The wind rushed through the field, and the shushing sound made its way to his ears in the most terrifying way. If he listened hard enough, he could imagine he heard words, the way he sometimes picked faces from the patterns in the wallpaper. His mind tried to make sense of the noise, and he swore that someone was saying his name. That the field knew who he was, and it was angry at him, and if he didn't hide, it would come for him in the dark. He hid under his sheets and waited for the rain to shut the whispers up.

Of all the things in the field, nothing terrified him more than Uncle Burle. No one could ever tell him who had named Uncle Burle. His father said it was his grandmother. His grandmother claimed it was her father. But however it had started didn't matter.

Uncle Burle was the scarecrow posted in the center of the field. Paul could see it night and day from his bedroom window. It faced the house, and he always imagined it was looking at him.

The scarecrow was made the way any other scarecrow might have been. It was mounted on a cross-shaped set of timbers, and the body was formed from a set of straw-stuffed denim overalls. The material had endured many a storm and was weather-beaten and well worn, but the denim was sturdy, and it held up over generations.

Beneath the overalls was an ancient plaid flannel shirt. It was red and white and reminded Paul of a tablecloth. Like the coveralls, it was stuffed to bulging with hay, and sometimes, his father had to bring Uncle Burle down and stuff it anew when weather or animals caused him to go limp.

An old straw hat was affixed on the scarecrow's head. Beneath it was a burlap sack, the origin of the scarecrow's name. The bag was stuffed with straw just like the body, and big, black Xs were stitched into it for eyes. The mouth was a series of smaller Xs, stitched with the same thick, black thread. He was neither smiling nor frowning; the stitches were a straight line across, making the scarecrow forever look disinterested.

When he was very young, Paul imagined it was Uncle Burle whispering in the storms. When he thought he heard his name, he feared it was the scarecrow calling out.

In his mind, Paul imagined that the scarecrow would capture him one day, and the burlap of its head would tear as it forced its mouth open, ripping the stitches until the bag was so wide it could open its jaws and swallow Paul whole. He would be dragged into the old, moldy straw and digested inside the coveralls, hanging from those timbers where no one would ever find him.

As he grew older, those fears subsided. He understood that the whispering was just the rough texture of those leaves rubbing together, the dry stalks and the husks creating friction. Uncle Burle was just unwanted old clothing and straw. It was just another mundane detail of life on the farm.

Paul was twenty-one, and his parents wanted him to do more with his life than they had, so they made sure he focused on his education above all else. But he worked the farm every day in the summer with his father.

He was the first in the family to go to college. He had a degree in biology and was pursuing a master's in agricultural engineering. He planned to ensure his education would still help the family and improve life for them and the other farmers he had known since he was a boy. That had been the plan, anyway.

The whispering from the corn was as loud as Paul had ever heard it. Sweat ran down his face, and he felt it warm and cloying around the collar of his shirt and down the small of his back. It was hard to breathe in the field. The rows seemed to close in on him and hold the humidity. The air was thick and clung to his face.

He knew the field like the back of his hand. He had seen it every day of his life for as long as he could remember. Except now, he couldn't find his way out. No matter how far he ran or how fast, the corn never ended.

He should have hit the house by now, or the road, or anything. Instead, there was only corn. The silky tops barely moved, showing there was no breeze and no reason for that whispering sound to be so loud. He couldn't see over anything. He couldn't find his way and had lost all sense of direction.

The sun was high in the sky. It was anchored dead center above him, so perfectly placed that he had no idea which way was east or west. If he could orient himself and guess the direction, he could leave. But nothing seemed to work.

The rows were planted from north to south. A run to the east or west should have freed him in minutes. But he had been in the field for more than half an hour without a sign of anything. It made no sense.

South of the field was the house. He had barely gone far enough to lose sight of it when he entered, following a shape that he thought was one of the local teens causing trouble. But nothing was what it should have been. And the whispering only grew louder.

The day was supposed to be hot, but the temperature in the cornfield was so much worse than Paul expected. It was stifling, and he feared that he would get heat stroke if he didn't find his way out soon.

He called out for help again and again but no one replied. His father had gone into town, his mother was in the house, and no one else was around. If his mother didn't come outside, no one would hear him. If he hadn't left his phone on the porch where he'd been sitting, he could have done something more. So many ifs.

Paul kept running. East or west, he would have to reach the edge of the field. It was much longer than it was wide, and he should get out sooner or later. He had to find a way out.

Dried leaves scratched at his skin as he passed between the stalks, moving row to row to get out. More time passed, too much time by far, and soon, he saw something. It was the first thing he had seen that wasn't corn since he entered the field. A shape in the near distance. He ran toward it.

He recognized the wooden pole before he reached it, the boots that hung a few feet off the ground, and the dark blue denim tucked into it. He had reached Uncle Burle.

The scarecrow hung stiff and silent, bits of straw poking out at the wrists around its gloves and under the burlap sack of its face above the collar of his shirt. Paul turned to face the same direction as the scarecrow. The corn was too high to see the house, but he knew it was there. The scarecrow was only about sixty yards from the edge of the porch.

He ran south with Uncle Burle at his back, focused on escaping and the flat, green lawn around the house that he knew would appear at any moment. The sun blazed down on his flesh, and the leaves rustled loudly, devoid of a breeze. He ran and ran and ran. The corn did not end.

Five minutes passed. It was impossible. He was no sprinter, but he was running. He should have reached the house three times over.

Paul cursed. He felt like he was losing his mind. Like he was caught in the most realistic dream he had ever experienced.

Several more minutes passed. Sweat covered Paul's face. He wiped his brow and kept running even as some made its way into his eyes, stinging and compromising his sight. He slowed down, stumbling as he used his sweaty, dirty hands to clean his eyes. When he lifted his head again, blinking to clear his vision, he saw a shape looming above him.

Blue denim coveralls. A red and white plaid shirt. The burlap face under the straw hat looking down at him with big, black X eyes.

"What the hell is going on?" he whispered.

Paul stared up at Uncle Burle, at the thick, black thread stitched into the loose weave of the old, brown burlap. The black X mouth was pulled taut around the edges and, as he watched, the thin, brown fibers pulled so tight that they snapped above and below the black Xs. The mouth tore itself open in a jagged split above and below the stitching, wherever the fibers were the weakest.

"Paulllllll," the scarecrow whispered.

Paul couldn't form words. For a heartbeat, he couldn't even move his body. He didn't believe what he saw. He couldn't because it was impossible.

Uncle Burle's arm rose slowly at its side. Paul heard the straw crinkling and snapping inside the limb as the gloved hand closed, forming a fist with only the index finger extended, pointing at Paul.

He turned and ran as the scarecrow moaned his name a second time. He made it only three paces before his feet got tangled in something thin and hard. Paul tripped and fell face-first into the dry soil, landing hard enough to give himself a nosebleed.

An old garden rake with thick, curved teeth was half-embedded in the dirt. He had tripped over the handle.

Paul wiped blood and muddy sweat from his face and looked back.

The cross-shaped timbers were still behind him, but Uncle Burle was not. There was no sign of the scarecrow.

He scrambled forward quickly, getting to his knees and then his feet as he put distance between himself and where the scarecrow had been. Within seconds, a scraping sound drew his attention back the way he had come.

Uncle Burle stood in the spot where Paul had just fallen. It held the rake in its gloved hand and slowly, loudly, scraped across the dry soil as it pursued him.

"Paullllll," the scarecrow moaned again, dragging the rake with one hand and reaching out for him with the other.

Paul ran, panic gripping him tightly and twisting in his guts. He did not know where to go or how to get out, and it didn't matter. He just needed to get away from the impossible thing calling his name.

The nightmares of his childhood flooded his mind, of the field and the burlap face speaking his name in secret, calling out to him as though accusing him of unknown crimes, and he wanted to scream. He wanted to call out for his mother and father and grandmother to make the sounds go away and make everything better. But this was not the nightmare of a little boy.

He dashed between stalks of corn, trying to put the straw-filled creature behind him and find the way out. Leaves slapped him in the face, the dry edges cutting his flesh and leaving stinging, bloody scrapes across his arms and cheeks and throat. His breath came in deep, struggling gasps as the humid air refused to fill his lungs.

The rake slashed out between rows and Paul reeled back, narrowly missing the curved, steel teeth. Uncle Burle stumbled forward, ahead of him once more, and stared down with black X eyes.

Paul was on his back, gasping in fear and exhaustion. The scarecrow lumbered forward and dragged the rake, lifting it slowly up and up as though raising an ax to bring down on a log.

Paul was too tired to run anywhere and too terrified to even get back to his feet. Paul simply stared in wide-eyed horror. He was going to die in the cornfield, and he knew it.

The sounds of metal scraping against metal rang out above the whispering leaves. Fire took hold of Uncle Burle's arm, and the scarecrow moaned, stumbling left and dropping the rake.

Paul watched as the fire consumed the dry straw and ancient fabric. Despite the humidity, the years of being exposed to the sun had made the scarecrow into a man-shaped tinderbox. Flames engulfed the body in minutes, and as the scarecrow fell to the ground, it revealed someone behind it.

Paul watched a scarred, bruised, bald man slip a Zippo into his pocket. He stared down at Paul, a plume of smoke rising from the cigarette in the man's mouth as the scarecrow shuddered and twisted in the fire.

"House is that way," the man said, pointing to his right. Paul looked at the writhing mass in the flames. "You should go."

The man kicked the burning scarecrow, and chunks of straw and burned clothing sloughed away as the fire petered out. There was something in the center of it, untouched by flames, and that was what the man focused on.

"Where the hell are the Harvesters?" the man asked, plucking the dark shape from the scarecrow's smoldering remains. "Where's Beatrix?"

The dark shape began to speak in a low, horrible voice, and Paul rolled over, scrambling to his feet and running before either the man or the thing he'd pulled from Uncle Burle thought to focus on him again.

Chapter 1
THE HUNT CONTINUES

Shane had the window down, and the breeze coming in pulled the ash from his cigarette, scattering it across his shoulder and then behind him into the car. He cursed quietly and brushed at his shoulder, making a mental note to clean the rear seat when he got home.

He would rest first, though. Maybe have something to eat and then sleep for a while. His body was not yet fully healed, not by a long shot, and he had strained himself more than he'd wanted to, tracking down the ghost in the cornfield and trying to get answers from it.

The wound on the back of his head had been cleaned, treated, and stitched up. The doctor told him he was lucky that he had a hard skull as the injury could have caused serious damage, even fatal if it had been much worse. As it was, he sustained a concussion and was taking antibiotics to ensure that it—and any of his other wounds—didn't get infected.

He still wasn't sure what had hit him in the head. He knew Beatrix's right-hand man Lanthimos had hit him. Lanthimos had bashed Shane's head at the cemetery, and they'd even buried him for his troubles.

Later, Lanthimos, Beatrix, and the ghost Cassius had taken a few rounds out of him. It was arguably one of the worst beatings Shane had ever received. Still, they'd messed up. They hadn't killed him. He wouldn't make the same mistake when he had the chance to repay their efforts.

Cassius was destroyed, but Beatrix and Lanthimos were still out there somewhere. So was whoever gave Beatrix her marching orders. It didn't matter who Beatrix was working with. Living or dead, Shane would make sure it ended the right way.

The doctors had not wanted him to leave the hospital. Neither had Agent Ventura. Ventura had helped keep Shane's name out of things when the law got involved. There was a trail of bodies and some destruction that needed to be accounted for, but thanks to Ventura's involvement, Shane was not a suspect.

Though Shane wouldn't have admitted it, he could have used some extra time to rest and heal. But Beatrix would not be resting. He couldn't afford to be doing nothing while she was still out there. It wasn't just the potential of what she could do next, and who she could hurt. Shane owed her now. She had started it with him, and he intended to finish it.

Ventura had not argued too hard against Shane heading out after her. He might have been young, and he was dealing with things he didn't fully understand, but he was smart enough to know Shane was better suited to handle someone like Beatrix than the FBI was. The law did not work in a way that allowed for the existence of ghosts.

The one concession that Ventura asked was that Shane keep him in the loop and let him help when he could. As much as Shane preferred doing things on his own and in his way, it was to his benefit to have Ventura in his corner. Ventura wasn't too pushy, and he didn't insist on being a part of things. That was the kind of partner Shane was happy to work with. One who stayed home.

Shane turned onto Berkley Street, heading toward his house. He'd come up emptyhanded after pursuing another lead in the hopes of finding Beatrix or the Harvesters. The ghost in the cornfield had not been very forthcoming. Either it knew nothing, or it was just tight-lipped, but Shane assumed the former. There was no reason for a spirit to show Beatrix any loyalty.

He had yet to come up with even a reasonable timeline for Beatrix's actions. It seemed like she had hunted ghosts for a couple of years at most, that was as far back in the timeline as he could track anything. Everything was so disjointed and disconnected. He couldn't even find out her last name or where she came from. Hell, he had no reason to believe Beatrix was even her real name.

There were two cars in front of his house when Shane pulled into the driveway. The house loomed over them, casting its shadow across the driveway and ensuring everyone was in darkness as he approached.

Most of the ghosts of the house were still hidden inside, not visible from the windows. This was par for the course. Carl, Eloise, and the others kept hidden whenever they could, especially during the day. Usually, anyway. Herbert was another matter.

Shane had befriended the ghost only a short time ago, and they had met Xander Ventura at the same time. Ventura and Herbert were outside, with Ventura leaning on the trunk of his car and talking to the enormous ghost while James Moran stood to one side.

Herbert was unlike the other spirits in the house. Carl had been a worldly man who had traveled Europe and the United States during his lifetime, and Eloise had been a gregarious child in life. In death, all the ghosts in the house on Berkley Street had one thing in common: they had almost always been in the house on Berkley Street. Even the Davis sisters had only been in one other place.

Herbert had traveled the country after his death. He'd moved around for decades as part of a carnival, never taking root anywhere and seeing new people every day for well more than an average lifespan. He was not accustomed to hiding when someone appeared, especially someone he knew.

Shane parked his car and got out, approaching the other men and the ghost.

"I'd say you look well, but that would be a very transparent lie," James said, shaking Shane's hand.

"Good to see you, too," he replied.

"Any luck in the cornfield?" Ventura asked.

"Found the ghost. He was trying to kill the farmer who lives there.

Possessed the scarecrow, of all things," Shane answered, lighting a new cigarette.

"That, I would love to have seen," Ventura said. "I didn't know ghosts could possess a non-living thing."

"Just wearing it like a suit," Shane said. "Makes the scares easier, I assume."

"There was a ghost at the carnival who sometimes possessed a marionette puppet after shows. He'd make the little wooden man walk around and chase children who strayed from their parents. Caused a lot of screams," Herbert said, pleased by the memory.

"Jesus," Ventura said. "That must have warped a few kids over the years."

"Perhaps," Herbert said with a shrug.

"In any case, he didn't know much," Shane continued. "Same story as the bog monster."

"There was a bog monster?" Ventura asked.

"Ah, well, not technically a bog monster. A ghost who drowned in a marsh," James corrected.

Shane gestured to the older man with his cigarette.

"They both ran through his shop once," Shane explained.

"Yes," James said. "The bog monster in question was a man named Flint. One of the more gruesome spirits I've seen over the years. Rotten, sagging flesh, unpleasant odor, a very living-dead, zombie feel to his appearance. That was part of the appeal for the buyer."

"Beatrix?" Ventura asked.

"Oh no, of course not. A man named Len Yulich. He purchased Flint's gold tooth more than a decade ago. Yulich, I've since learned, was murdered. His property was stolen, and the gold tooth was taken with some other items."

"Like Benedict Winston," Ventura interjected.

Winston was the man who'd owned Cassius and a ghost named

August. August had mailed himself to James looking for help after Beatrix and the Harvesters killed Winston and released Cassius for the fun of hunting him. More than a dozen people died because of their hunt before Shane destroyed the spirit.

"Much the same, it seems. And the spirit from the cornfield seems to have been sold to Benjamin Putter close to twenty years ago."

"Is Putter dead?" Ventura asked.

"He is. More than a year ago. I was told it was an accident, but I wonder how true that is considering these other cases," James said.

"I can look into them," Ventura said, writing names in a small notebook. "I don't have much else to go with on my end, though."

"Nothing on Beatrix?" Shane asked.

"No. I pulled what I could on her two dead associates from the fish factory, Kraft and Tully. Minor stuff. Tully was involved in an assault and battery three years back. Kraft was questioned as a witness to a murder but was never a suspect. Nothing that linked one to the other."

"They murdered people, didn't they?" Herbert asked.

"We've got a murder victim and fingerprints from the deceased in his house. August was our witness, and he's both a ghost and destroyed. Cassius committed all the other murders. In the real world, I can't bring charges against anyone for any of this. I need Beatrix, and the gun she used, or another witness."

"Doesn't matter. We're not looking to prosecute anyone," Shane pointed out.

"Maybe not," Ventura agreed, "but in terms of helping you find these people or cover your ass if more bodies turn up, it's hard to do with so many holes to patch up. I can't tell my director that a ghost is the reason we haven't brought in a suspect."

"Frustrating though that might be, I'm more concerned with what links these three murders. Winston, Yulich, and Putter. How did Beatrix know them? How did she find their hidden ghosts, and why did she let all of them loose?" James said.

"How did you find them again?" Ventura asked.

"Witnesses. People talk in my line of work. There are only so many spirits that look like Flint. But he was in a different state from where Yulich lived."

"Found him in a school," Shane told Ventura. "Harassing some local kids having a party."

"Harassing?"

Shane shrugged.

"Might have planned to kill them; I don't know. Didn't get that far. Beatrix releases the ghosts to hunt them; it's what she did with Cassius. I assume she released these other two for similar reasons."

"But she abandoned them," Ventura said. "Why do that?"

"From what I saw, this woman likes two things: Money and hunting, and they seem to go together. If the hunter doesn't pay, I don't think she finishes the job."

"It makes sense in a way," James said. "Suppose you pay her to take you on a ghost hunt, and then you realize you're in over your head. Or maybe you get killed. She could leave the ghost and reuse it later. Get someone else to pay her for it."

"Phelps said she had a list of ghosts to choose from. He chose Cassius because it was local. The others could have been ones she already released," Shane said. "She wouldn't care if these things killed a hundred people while she wrangled up a new paying customer."

"That's deranged," Ventura said.

Shane chuckled and nodded, exhaling smoke.

"Yeah."

"So, our girl knows who collects ghosts, and somehow, which ghosts they collected. Even obscure ones or ones that have been kept secret like this Cassius. What's the common thread?" Ventura asked.

"I've been trying to figure that out," James said.

"Aside from you, I suppose," the agent added.

James looked at him with narrowed eyes.

"I am not involved in this, Agent Ventura," the old man said bluntly. Ventura held up his hands.

"Didn't mean to suggest you were, Mr. Moran. But all three dead men were your clients."

"Years ago," James agreed. "And none were involved with the others. I didn't even sell Winston the spirit they stole from him."

"No," Ventura said, "but you're still a link. This is a niche world, isn't it? So, who else would know all three men? Who else could connect A, B, and C? You can't be the only one."

James went quiet and Shane finished his cigarette. He wouldn't have said it quite as awkwardly as Ventura had, but the thought had also occurred to him. He didn't suspect James Moran of anything illicit, and he believed that the man had no idea who Beatrix was. But that didn't mean he wasn't a link in the chain. He had clients and colleagues, any of whom could have been involved and indirectly pulled him into something.

"You keep your records secure, right?" Ventura asked then.

"Of course. My files are under lock and key. My clients demand discretion."

"But would a ghost be deterred by a locked filing cabinet?"

"Ghosts cannot steal files from a locked cabinet. And none of mine are missing. I checked into this when I found out who had died and what business we'd done."

"But could a ghost read them?" Ventura said.

Shane could see the tension in the corner of James' eyes. He hadn't thought of that because what ghost would break into an office to read paperwork? It would have been a stupid suggestion if it hadn't at least sounded plausible.

"I only know what I've been able to unearth," James said. He sounded confident, but there was something there. Shane could see he was shaken.

Maybe Ventura or Herbert couldn't, but Shane had known James Moran long enough to see something had changed.

"What have you got?" Shane asked.

CHAPTER 2
THE FUNDAMENTALS OF DEATH

"Little more than I've already told you," James began.

The shadow of the house was cold, despite the heat of the day. The breeze rolled in hot and humid and then died down as the cool of the shadow set in once more.

Shane could see movement in the windows behind the other men. He drew no attention to it, but the time he'd spent in the driveway had piqued the others' curiosity. Carl watched from the third floor, while Eloise and the Davis sisters caused curtains to stir on the ground floor. None would come outside, he suspected. They were not comfortable enough with Ventura to expose themselves so openly. But everyone was paying attention.

Beatrix had already sent a package to the house once. She knew where Shane lived, meaning everyone was compromised. The others were invested in what had happened. They had all offered to help, to leave the safety of the home and travel with him to fight her. He'd turned them all down and wound up in the hospital. That put them all on edge, even more than usual.

"I've been able to identify a few other one-time clients who have died or gone missing in the past ten years, and it seems like their homes were also robbed of specific haunted items. Only one appears to have been a murder, though the police arrested a suspect. But the details are similar enough that it drew my attention," James explained, handing some paperwork to Shane.

"These are ghosts?" Shane asked, leafing through the pages.

"Yes. I traced the spirits back to the owners and discovered that all had passed away. One was from an item I sold to the former owner; the others had items I sold them, but these spirits were not from me. In each of these cases, the relevant spirit, one I would consider highly dangerous and unsafe in the hands of anyone who had not been well-vetted, has been moved to a new, unrestrained location."

"Same thing they did with Cassius and these other ones," Ventura said.

"Most of them are near where they were originally kept. Only one crossed state lines," James continued.

"So, the Harvesters identify a ghost, kill the owner, capture the spirit, and release it for a hunt. If someone pays for the hunt, it goes down as planned. If they can't pay or it's otherwise derailed, the ghost is left to run free until someone else wants to pony up the cash to take it down. That's our working theory?" Ventura asked.

"Seems like," Shane replied.

"The evidence points in that direction," James agreed. "I'm sure we're still missing some of the finer details."

"Like how they learn about the spirits to begin with," Shane said. He lifted the sheaf of papers James had handed him. "But maybe one of these knows."

"Give me the names of the other dead collectors, and I'll see what links I can dig up," Ventura suggested.

James glanced at Shane, who nodded, and the older man quickly scrawled some names on a page in a notebook and handed it to the agent.

"After this, I'm afraid my well of information has run dry. I have word out among other collectors. No one has told me anything about the Harvesters yet, but that can't last. If they have been running hunts for some time, someone will have either partaken or at least looked into it. I'm confident I'll find someone," James said.

"Maybe you can dig up something else," Shane said. "Either one of you. Beatrix had ghosts with her. They were like hunting dogs. I've seen some strange spirits before, and some monstrous ones, but these were engineered. Someone bred these things."

Ventura's eyebrow raised, and he gave James a sidelong glance before refocusing his attention on Shane.

"I know I'm the new kid here, but I'm going to need you to explain that," he said.

"I'm not sure I understand what you mean, either," James added.

"She had a few of them with her at Winston's," Shane explained. "They were badly deformed. Every bone was broken and reset so they were running on all fours, but with a half-dozen new joints in each limb. Their faces had been skinned, but in patterns. It was like a design, carefully carved in the flesh. Surgical."

"Some ghosts come back after enduring severe trauma, right? They look ugly sometimes," Ventura said.

"These weren't ugly ghosts," Shane said. "Someone did this to living people. They kept them alive long enough to break their bones. They flayed their skulls but kept them alive long enough to do it."

"So, there is a deranged killer out there," Ventura said.

Shane shrugged. That was true, but the agent wasn't getting it.

"Not everyone comes back as a ghost. Not everyone comes back as a certain kind of ghost, either. Carl looks like he did when he was alive. So does Herbert," Shane pointed out.

"Minus an arm," the big ghost added, indicating the stump of the appendage he'd lost after he died.

"Point is, you can't predict a ghost's appearance. You can't make a ghost as far as I know. It's a crapshoot. So, if Beatrix kills a guy by breaking all his bones and flaying his skull, odds are he's going to just be dead."

Ventura looked at James. Shane could see he understood what he was saying, even if the younger FBI agent wasn't quite there.

"That's terrifying," James said.

"What is?" Ventura asked.

"There are no odds I can offer you, Agent Ventura, on becoming a ghost. It's not as simple as saying fifty percent of the dead return. Or five percent. There is little rhyme or reason. For someone to breed ghosts the way Shane is describing... I can't imagine how many failures they would produce before achieving a single success."

Shane could see it click in Ventura's mind.

"Each failure is a person. Someone they're torturing and killing."

"Torturing worse than anything I've ever seen," Shane said. "And she just threw them at me. I had to destroy them. But James is right. How many people died before they made even one, let alone the three I saw? Dozens, at least."

"Are there more?" Ventura asked.

"That's what I want to know," Shane said.

It was a sour note to end on, but business had run its course. No one had anything new to add, so the three men could only go forward with what they had shared and do their respective jobs.

James and Ventura would return to where they had come from and continue their research. Shane had a list of places to visit; the ghosts James had tracked down. Like the bog monster and the scarecrow before them, Shane would see what, if anything, he could learn from them. The first two had been less than forthcoming with information, but eventually, someone would have to know something.

If their working theory was correct, Shane was culling the herd for the Harvester's hunts. They would run out of ghosts to offer clients, which would cut off their funds moving forward. If he couldn't track Beatrix, he could at least get her angry enough to come after him.

"Let me know if you discover anything," Ventura said.

"Will do," Shane said.

The agent nodded, then turned to Herbert and extended a hand. Herbert looked at it and chuckled. Ventura dropped it awkwardly.

"Right. I'll remember one day. Good to see you, Herbert."

"You too, Xander," the ghost said.

Ventura got into his car and pulled out, driving off with a quick wave. James Moran waited only a moment longer, pausing to speak with Shane before he got into his vehicle.

"Those spirits are quite dangerous," he said, gesturing to the pages he'd given Shane.

"I'd expect nothing less," Shane said.

James smiled and shrugged.

"It's not that I don't think you can handle yourself; you know that. But I'm not speaking out of turn in suggesting you're not in peak form right now."

Shane had to laugh. James wasn't wrong; he was not at his best. Unfortunately, no one could stop the clock to let him rest and feel better before he headed back out. As it was, he felt like he was taking things too slow.

"I'll watch my six," Shane said.

"Of course," James replied. They shook hands, and the older man got in his vehicle.

Shane and Herbert watched him leave, standing side by side in the driveway as Shane lit another cigarette.

"Are you well enough to keep this up?" Herbert asked. There was no sense of judgment in the question; he was merely curious. Shane found the ghost's lack of familiarity with him and the way things usually worked oddly refreshing.

"Don't have much of a choice," Shane said.

"I could come with you. Our last adventure was memorable."

"It was. But that time we weren't facing off against a woman who could pop your head like a balloon."

"No, just a town full of ghosts who could have."

"Not the same," Shane said. "And you're worse off than I am. You going to arm-wrestle her to death?"

Herbert laughed and nodded.

"Maybe you're right. I'm no warrior. But you have options. Carl seems coldly efficient to me."

"He is," Shane agreed. "But he was kidnapped from the house just a short time before you arrived. The man deserves a rest."

"It sounds like you're making excuses," Herbert said.

"I'm not. I don't need an excuse because I don't plan to bring anyone with me. This is just polite banter while I finish my cigarette."

"Naturally," Herbert said. "Figured I could at least try."

"Noble effort," Shane told him.

He exhaled a puff of smoke and Herbert looked back at the house.

"I don't want to overstep my bounds. I'm new and maybe naïve in some ways. But you look like you very nearly died. Is it pride that pushes you? Hate? You have to be realistic about your limitations. You are, after all, still alive."

Shane sighed and didn't look at the ghost. New and naïve he was, indeed.

"It's *need*," Shane answered. "This needs to be done. I'll heal. Or I won't. It doesn't matter. People drop like flies wherever this woman goes. And these things... these broken ghosts she uses. Dozens of dead is a lowball, Herbert. To craft a ghost is only considered impossible because of how insane you would have to be to make it work. To kill countless people to produce one perfectly deranged monster is something I can barely imagine, and I can imagine a lot."

Herbert nodded slowly. Shane was not sure if the ghost understood. From Herbert's perspective, returning as a ghost was not remarkable. He was one, and he had met many others. To appreciate the rarity of it, and then compound that by making some kind of bespoke monster, was staggering.

"I don't want to sound like I'm delving into your motives or feelings because it's not my place," Herbert began again. "But does the fact that this Beatrix woman can do what you do have something to do with why you're so eager to find her?"

"Not trying to delve into my motives, huh?" Shane replied.

He understood what the ghost was getting at. Of course, it was a mitigating factor that he couldn't overlook. She was, in the most rudimentary way, a mirror of himself.

Beatrix could have chosen a different path. She could have been a hundred different people. But she chose to be a killer. She chose to be a danger to anyone who crossed her path. And she did so using the same skills Shane possessed, skills that almost no one else in the world had. He took it personally. He couldn't help it.

Shane finished his cigarette, pinched out the butt, and turned toward the house.

"Are you angry?" Herbert asked.

"More annoyed than angry. Too tired to be angry," Shane replied. "But not at you. Either way, I need some sleep before I go after these new targets."

"Good idea," Herbert said, following him back.

CHAPTER 3
UNWANTED GIFTS

"Is everything well?" Carl asked.

He stood in front of the grandfather clock inside the entrance to the house. Shane nodded and made his way to the kitchen while Carl and Herbert followed. Eloise was there when he arrived, as were two of the Davis sisters. The third must have been somewhere nearby, but he could not see her.

"Did you kill her?" Eloise asked.

"Not yet," Shane said. He filled a glass with water and stood next to the sink drinking it.

"You should kill her," Daphne suggested.

"Soon," Dora added.

"We could help," Daisy said. She joined Shane on his other side, appearing from beyond the wall.

"Everyone's eager to get in on this one," he said. "Real family-vacation vibe you're all giving."

"We are just concerned, my young friend," Carl said, his voice unusually soft.

Shane grunted and finished his water.

"If I need help, I'll be sure to let everyone know," he said.

He left the glass in the sink and walked out of the kitchen. He wasn't sure what had brought on this uncharacteristic round of concern from the ghosts in the house. Not that Carl and the others were unconcerned historically, but this was different.

He had been injured in the past; quite badly, in fact. A brush with death was nothing new for Shane, and it shouldn't have been anything new to the ghosts. If anything, Herbert should have been the one surprised by it, and he seemed to be taking it easier than the older spirits who should have known better.

Herbert had also brought up another possibility. It wasn't Shane that they were all concerned about. It was Beatrix, or more specifically what she represented. She was another Shane to them. Another person who could destroy the dead. She was a threat, an existential one.

They were used to Shane bearing the brunt of the danger in any given circumstance. This was something new for everyone. And since she had already made a threat against the house, everyone was on edge.

Shane supposed he should cut them some slack. They had every right to feel afraid, or nervous. He just wished they would feel that way without clustering around him and offering advice or assistance when he hadn't requested it. That was not the nature of their relationship, and he didn't want it to start being that way.

He headed to his room and closed the door, enjoying some privacy for a moment. Since his stay in the hospital, he'd been pushing himself harder than he should have, and he knew it.

He didn't want to accept that he needed to take more time than he had available, but what he wanted didn't matter. He had to accept that he wasn't going to be operating at one hundred percent. Everyone else just had to accept that he wasn't going to give up or wait.

Beatrix and the Harvesters had injured him, but they hadn't defeated him. He would just have to be smarter about how he approached them going forward. There were plenty of ways to win a fight that didn't involve getting circle-booted in a motel parking lot. He'd use one of those.

After using the restroom, Shane laid on his bed and closed his eyes, relishing the brief moment of relaxation. There was something about that first instance of lying down that always felt profound to him. The ability to relax, if only just, was something special.

Every muscle in his body felt tense. The very act of letting them loosen felt like it took effort. Like it was his body's natural state to forever be on edge. It had seeped into his bones. It was just the way things were, and he only got these brief moments of respite.

The air in the room was warm, and he felt like he was sinking into the mattress. He would rest for a short while and then get back to it. He would follow James' leads, find the ghosts, and stop Beatrix.

One thing at a time, though.

✳✳✳

Shane opened his eyes as something cold and firm pressed down hard over his face. The room was much darker than it had been when he closed his eyes what felt like only a moment earlier.

He had fallen asleep, and now he awoke harshly and unexpectedly. The cold pressure over his face held him down, and he blinked at the darkness of his room, focusing on the figure hovering over him.

"Someone is here."

Eloise looked down at him, her hand covering his mouth. She whispered the words close to his ear, pulling away when she saw that he was awake and had heard what she was saying.

There was an unexpected silence in the house, more than usual. He realized what was missing when he looked at the clock next to his bed and could not see the display. The power was out. The background hum of electricity was gone, and the house was as still as a grave.

"Who?" Shane whispered.

As if in response, the house began to rumble. It was slow and subtle at first, a vibration that worked up through the floor into the bed under Shane. He felt it even as he heard the soft clatter of debris falling inside the walls.

Windows rattled in their frames and objects on tabletops wobbled and shook. The house groaned, it seemed like a small earthquake at first. But Shane knew better. He knew no one else in Nashua felt what he did just then. The house was moving.

Eloise shook her head, indicating she had no idea who had invaded their home. Someone was there who didn't belong, and the house was alerting everyone to the unwanted presence. Shane had never witnessed it react so violently, though.

Of course, the house could do things on its own. Shane was not the only one who opened a door to discover a room on the other side that shouldn't have been there. And he knew the house could make a fourth floor appear and disappear seemingly at random. But for the whole house to react, for it to shake from the foundation, was not usual.

Shane was out of bed and at the door before the rumble subsided. The hall beyond his room was pitch black. Carl appeared in moments with Herbert behind him. Both spirits glowed faintly, almost imperceptibly, but enough to allow them to stand out in the darkness of the house at night.

"Something broke in," Carl said. "It moves swiftly. It is not alive."

Before Shane could ask for clarification, something clicked and rattled on the stairs at the end of the hall. Shane focused on it, his eyes adjusting to the ambient light. The top of the stairs was a shadow within shadows, just shapes and shades of black, but he could make it out well enough to know where it was.

Shane identified a pale head first. There was no hair, and the flesh looked white in the way a drowning victim sometimes became like a fish's belly. But while the pale head had flesh on top, a strip was missing that extended from above the eyebrows to the bridge of the nose across the eyes.

At least three inches of tissue had been cut away in a perfectly straight line. There were no eyes in the sockets, just empty, black holes in a skull. Shane knew what it was before the rest of the monstrosity came into view.

"What is that?" Herbert whispered. "Is that one of the things you told

Xander about?"

The Hound clambered up the steps on rickety, broken limbs. Even in the dark, Shane could see that the ghost's arms were bending in multiple places where it should not have had joints. The bones had been broken again and again to allow for the creature to be formed as it was. The legs were no different, with the knees bent in the wrong direction.

Along the ghost's back were random fragments of bone that jutted out, as well as pieces of what might have been rock or glass, though it was hard to tell. Like the ones that Shane had encountered, the deformed creature climbing his steps had endured untold suffering to forge it into something nature had never dreamed of creating.

The empty eyes stared down the hall at Shane and the ghosts. He could feel its gaze in his gut and knew that it saw him, and that it had been sent for him by Beatrix.

"Come on, then," Shane said to it. "Let's get this over with."

The ghost opened its mouth as though to scream, but all that came out was a rattling sound from somewhere deep within its body. It bounded away from the stairs and loped down the hallway toward Shane. Its rubbery limbs bent and curved in impossible ways, allowing it to run as though it had been born to a four-legged gait.

Shane cut it off just before it had a chance to jump at him, taking three strides toward it to ensure it had no upper hand when they met. He crashed into the ghost, tackling it with his full weight and throwing it to the floor of the hallway.

The ghost fought like the others, all four limbs striking, bending, swiping, and doing anything to entangle Shane and allow the ghost to overpower him.

His prior experience told him that the broken limbs were too flexible to bother controlling. The trade-off was that, although they had been granted a wider range of movement than any living creature, their attacks were not as strong as they could have been.

Shane ignored the arms and legs and focused on the body and head. He held the ghost down and punched it in the face, forcing it to turn its head long enough that he hooked a thumb into its empty eye and got a grip on the skull.

The ghost was strong and not willing to give up so quickly. It grabbed at Shane's back with both hands and pulled him away, causing him to lose his grip on the skull. He saw Carl and Eloise from the corners of his eyes, wanting to intervene but also not wanting to risk harm.

"Stay back," he told them. There was no point in them getting involved. It was his fight. "Watch out for more."

The ghost pulled him away by the back of his shirt and threw him against the wall. He recovered quickly but so did the Hound, getting onto its hands and feet once again so that it could square off with Shane like an attack dog.

Carl and Eloise were reluctant to listen, but he saw them drift off to check the rest of the house and ensure that no more of the Hounds had been sent after them.

The walls shook and rumbled, and Shane watched as wooden boards buckled and bowed like they might shatter at any moment, and the house would fall apart around him.

The deformed ghost took another run at him, and he caught it around the neck, ignoring the hands as they beat and battered his sides and legs, focusing instead on squeezing the dead thing's neck and forcing it down to the ground once more. The ghost clawed, kicked, and even gnashed its teeth, but Shane drove a fist into its spine, punching it again and again until it collapsed to its stomach while he straddled its back.

With the ghost face-down, Shane clutched its head between his hands and began to squeeze. Something hit him in the back of the head, knocking him forward and sending a wave of pain through the injury he had previously sustained. The ghost had bent its leg completely backward and kicked him, allowing itself to get up once more.

Their fight went back and forth, with Shane thinking he had the upper hand only to discover the ghost's broken form allowed it to break free and turn the tables on him.

His body was tired and sore, and the fight was not getting easier. He hadn't expected Beatrix to do him any favors and give him time to prepare for a fair fight, though. That was not how this would play out. He had to fight through the discomfort.

Shane and the ghost collided again, now at the top of the stairs. The ghost rolled them over and gained the advantage. Its knees pinned Shane at the waist, and the broken arms reached out, the icy hands clutching at Shane's wrists to hold them at bay.

Hollow sockets stared into his eyes and pale, bloated lips parted to expose stained and broken teeth. The ghost spread its jaw wide and leaned in, aiming for Shane's throat.

CHAPTER 4
INVITATION

Shane struggled in the ghost's grip. It showed no sign of weakening or losing interest in its target. The ghost's mouth spread impossibly wide, indicating even the jaw had been broken and set incorrectly, just like the arms and legs. It was nearly unhinged like a snake's, broken teeth exposed.

A hand got in the way, pushing between Shane and the spirit. Slender, pale fingers slipped over the jagged teeth and gripped the jaws. Two more hands slipped around the back of the ghost head, clutching the upper jaw, and pulling the head back.

A fourth hand joined, this one clutching at the ghost's neck, and then a fifth hand snaked around Shane's head and plunged its fingers into the ghost's body right above the collarbone.

"Can't have this," Dora said.

She pulled and twisted, working the Hound's lower jaw the way someone might pull a chicken thigh off an uncooked bird. The joints popped and something tore.

Behind the ghost, Daisy pulled back on its head, snapping the spirit's back in the process as she knelt on its spine while Daphne reached both hands into its torso, snaking her fingers beneath the collarbone on either side of its chest and pulling the bones free.

In one coordinated movement, all three sisters attacked. The ghost's neck, jaw, and collarbone snapped as one.

Daisy pulled the broken thing off Shane while Daphne tossed fragments of bone away, causing the ghost's arms to hang limp from the damage across its shoulders.

Shane got to his feet just as Dora plunged a hand into the ghost's face, hooking fingers through the empty eye sockets like she was gripping a bowling ball. With her sisters providing extra leverage on the body, she broke the ghost's face from its skull.

All three sisters hurled the ghost down the stairs as it came apart. The body burst like an overfilled balloon, and two simultaneous blasts vibrated off the walls of the house, causing another small quake.

"Unwelcome guests are horrid," Daphne said to Shane.

"Repulsive," Daisy added.

"Are you well?" Dora finished, smiling at Shane as though nothing had just happened.

"I'm fine," he said. "Are there more?"

"There are more?" Daisy asked.

"We should kill them," Daphne suggested.

"Yes, I would like to do that again," Dora said.

"One step at a time," Shane advised, heading down the stairs with the sisters and Herbert in tow. If there were more, Carl and Eloise would have found them by now. He heard nothing from elsewhere in the house, even as he searched from room to room.

"Where are they?" he asked the others.

The search only lasted for two rooms before Carl presented himself, coming to Shane through a wall.

"I see nothing else on the grounds," he said.

"Eloise?" Shane asked. Carl shook his head just as Herbert pointed to the front of the house.

"There," he said.

The ghost of the little girl appeared in the hallway, coming toward them with an especially sour look on her face.

"A package was left at the door," she said. "But I could not find who left it."

"Another box?" Shane asked.

The ghost nodded. Beatrix had left a box for him before. That time it was nothing, just a threat to let him know she knew where he was. This time was obviously meant to get his full attention.

He proceeded to the front door and opened it, stepping out into the cool night air to look around. If Eloise had said she couldn't find who left it, they were probably gone before the broken ghost had even invaded the house. He doubted Beatrix dropped it herself. She probably sent one of her Harvesters to do it, and they had fled the moment the job was done.

The ghost was not meant to kill Shane. Not that Beatrix would have felt bad about it succeeding, but he didn't suspect that she expected it to work. It was just meant to unsettle him. It was meant to remind him that she was still out there.

If he got injured in the fight, then so be it, but she was not dumb enough to think a late-night visit from one ghost would accomplish anything other than making him angry. That was the kind of petty act he expected from her.

The package at the front door was in a poor state. It was still wrapped in paper, but it looked like someone had stomped on it. The paper was torn, and the box inside was broken. With one final look around, he bent to pick up the box and returned to the house.

Unlike the previous box, this one had no lead plates inside. That made sense, of course, as it was designed to transport a spirit, not trap one. It weighed very little, but Shane was forced to carry it in two hands as it threatened to fall to pieces otherwise.

There was enough light coming through the kitchen window that he could place it on the table and see what he was doing. The already-torn paper pulled away easily, revealing the remnants of a destroyed wooden box within.

Beatrix had provided another handwritten note inside the box along with what appeared to be a shattered pair of glasses. The glasses would have been the haunted item that bound the spirit the Davis sisters had destroyed. After they tore him apart, the glasses were destroyed as well, damaging the box and the note that Beatrix had sent with it.

Despite the damage, the note was still legible. She had folded it over several times and used a small length of string to tie it up. She must have anticipated what would happen and did her best to ensure that he would still be able to read it once he was finished with the spirit.

Shane pulled off the string and unrolled the note. The handwriting was the same as the previous message Beatrix had sent. This one, however, was much simpler. It read:

Thinking of you.

He tossed it on the table. The others could read it clearly enough, but none of them remarked on it.

"I think whoever left it drove away. I saw lights but not the car," Eloise explained.

"Doesn't matter," Shane said.

"I've never seen a ghost like that," Carl said.

Carl had been trapped in the house since his death, but in life, he had been all around the world. He had seen more than his fair share of ghosts in his line of work as well, mediating disputes between the living and the dead. He was right, though. Shane doubted many people had seen spirits like the ones that Beatrix sent after him. They were unique nightmares. Most people never would have thought about creating something like that.

"What if she comes back?" Herbert asked. "She could have more, right?"

"She probably does," Shane said. "But they won't be back tonight."

"If they find out you're still alive, they might," Eloise said.

Shane shook his head.

"This wasn't about killing me. Beatrix would have come herself if she wanted me dead. This was just to let me know that she hasn't forgotten."

"So, what will you do?" Carl asked.

"I'm going to destroy every ghost she has. I'll end her hunt until she only has one target left. Me."

"Take us with you. I'll kill her before she lets another one of those monsters loose," Eloise said.

"We can break more of them," Daisy said excitedly.

"Into pieces," Dora added.

"Dead and forever," Daphne finished.

"I don't need help," Shane said.

"You needed it this time," Herbert pointed out.

Shane locked eyes with the big ghost, and even the Davis sisters seemed to tense up. Shane could see Carl in his peripheral vision shaking his head slowly as if telling Herbert to back off. The big ghost had not meant it the way it had come across, and Shane told himself that Herbert was new. He was naïve.

"When I say I don't need help, it's not an offer for a debate," Shane replied.

"I didn't mean to—"

"Nor is it an offer to continue the discussion," Shane added, cutting him off. "I don't need to take anyone with me. What I do need is for you to stay here. Beatrix hunts ghosts. She kills their owners and steals them. She'll take them someplace and let them loose so someone can pay her to hunt them. If she knows where I live, there's every reason to believe she knows each one of you in this house."

"You're saying we're in danger, too?" Herbert asked.

"Of course," Shane told him. "If you think there are rules to her fight, then you're already one step behind her. She's not going to play fair. She won't have sympathy or mercy. When she sticks a knife in, she twists it, and she'll do it every time. If she comes here when I'm gone, you're going to need to be ready for her."

"How?" Herbert asked. "If she's like you, how can we fight that?"

"Do you expect us to hide?" Carl asked.

"You can't," Shane said. "Beatrix doesn't work alone. The Harvesters are a team. They can all see ghosts, but more than that, they can track them. They have technology that makes it impossible for you to stay hidden, even within the walls, even when you think you're out of sight. They will know where you are. They have weapons that can stun you, and Beatrix will get rid of any of you that she doesn't want."

"I'll kill them before they get a chance," Eloise said.

Shane turned to the little girl and nodded.

"You'll have to. All of you will. This isn't a fight you can avoid or sit out. If she shows up with the Harvesters, with more of those broken ghosts, don't hesitate. If I'm not here, it's going to be on you. You're literally fighting for your life, even if you don't have one anymore. Don't forget that."

He looked around the room, catching the eye of every ghost in turn to make sure they heard his words and understood their weight. He was not convinced Beatrix would take the step of attacking the house while he was gone, but she had proven herself entirely unpredictable. Whatever made sense didn't matter when dealing with Beatrix. That meant preparing for everything and expecting something else.

"Why not stay here then?" Herbert asked. "Isn't this note just baiting you to go look for her?"

"Maybe," Shane said. "But I'm not looking for her right now. I'm looking for her ghosts. I know where to go. The hunt is the only thing she seems to care about, and the money that comes along with it. If I take that away, I'll get her attention. It's about time she felt what it's like to be against the ropes."

"Don't worry, Shane. We'll kill anyone who comes through the door," Daphne said proudly.

"Everyone," Dora corrected.

"Yes. They'll all die screaming," Daisy finished.

The sisters were excited by the idea of facing the Harvesters, but the others had taken a much more reserved attitude to the situation. Carl, of course, always had a measured response. Herbert looked the least convinced of his ability to fight off Beatrix and the Harvesters, for good reason. He was down an arm, and he was not a fighter at the best of times. Shane felt like he knew the ghost well enough to know that he would do what he could, though.

"And you?" Shane asked, looking at Eloise.

"What about me?"

"Are you ready?"

"Oh, please, Shane Ryan. I'm always ready."

CHAPTER 5
TURNING THE TABLES

Shane's instinct was to leave immediately, hit the road, and do as much damage to Beatrix's bottom line as he could as fast as he could. But he knew he had to be smarter than that. It was still late, so he headed back to his room.

Under other circumstances, he might have headed out, but he needed the rest, so he took advantage of the time he had. Despite the stress of the situation and his lack of certainty that he'd be able to get back to sleep, he surprised himself. He vaguely remembered closing his eyes, and the next thing he knew, sunlight was streaming through his window.

Shane had a quick coffee in the morning and a bite to eat before heading out again. Carl assured him that the house would be taken care of in his absence, and that if Beatrix or her Hounds returned, they would regret it. Shane hoped that was true.

He didn't doubt Carl's sincerity or his abilities. But Beatrix was formidable. She was good at what she did.

James Moran had provided Shane with several addresses, or at least general areas where he could look for stolen ghosts. The closest was in Greenfield, Massachusetts. Shane hit the road not long after sunrise.

He wasn't going to lie to himself and pretend like he was fine. Shane knew he was not at one hundred percent, but he had used his time wisely. He felt stronger than he had the day before. He felt well-rested. Time was doing what it did, and he would be back at peak strength soon enough.

The drive to Greenfield took nearly two hours. He stopped for another coffee along the way and drove with the windows down, enjoying the fresh air and the breeze that came with it.

James' information about the ghost was limited but adequate. Shane didn't need a life story, he just needed a location. The spirit he was looking for had originally come from Boston. The man who once had it in his possession had died a couple of years earlier. The ghost was spotted a year after that, at a motel in Greenfield.

The place was called the Wagon Train Inn, and it was located off the highway about ten minutes outside of Greenfield proper. The lot was set back from the road and abandoned. There was a Western motif despite its location in the middle of Massachusetts. From the outside, it was clear that no one had stayed in the motel in at least half a decade, probably longer.

There was a statue of a horse out front, and the signboard had been stripped and broken. The parking lot was overgrown with weeds, and all the windows that weren't boarded up were broken.

Shane pulled off the main road and drove up the bumpy, pothole-laden path to the overgrown parking lot at around nine in the morning. Cars zipped past on the highway behind him, no one pausing to take a second glance at the rundown relic of a motel that passed them in the blink of an eye.

The office of the motel was designed to look like a saloon, and there were wagon wheels and barnboard and Old West decorations attached to the walls outside the rooms. Most were cracked and sun-bleached, but Shane couldn't have imagined the place looking authentic even in its prime.

He parked his car near the office and got out, looking around the lot at the rundown building, wondering where to start. There was no sign of movement in the few windows he could see through. The sound of cars rushing past on the highway overwhelmed any sound that might have come from the motel, but he didn't suspect there was anything to hear. The place was as dead as any graveyard he'd been in.

Shane tried the office door, jiggling the rusty handle, which felt loose but wouldn't give. The door was locked. With a shrug, he kicked it in. It seemed unlikely anyone would care.

Inside the office was a desk, a board that had once held keys, piles of water-damaged pamphlets on the counter, and an old, dirty carpet. It smelled stale and dusty all around, and when he walked around the counter, there was nothing to see in the back room. The place had been gutted, and no one had been there in years.

He headed next to the first guestroom and found the door similarly locked. Another swift kick opened it up. Unlike the office, this room smelled of mold and mildew. The dampness was heavy, and it looked like the ceiling had a serious leak.

A queen-sized mattress on a broken bed frame sat swollen with moisture. The stink coming off it was almost unbelievable, and the edges were black with layers of mold. Shane covered his nose and looked around him. Nothing moved or seemed out of place. The air was warm and unpleasant. If there was a ghost in there, it was well-hidden. He walked away, heading back to the parking lot and fresher air.

The next room didn't even have a door. Someone had squatted there for a time, from the looks of things. There was evidence that a fire had been set in the middle of the room, and the bed was missing. Old trash was piled up in the corner, including beer cans, fast food wrappers, and drug paraphernalia.

Shane traveled from room to room. Some had suffered leaks, but none as bad as the first one. Some had been gutted, with even the countertops pulled away and the cupboard doors ripped from the walls.

It was a hot day, and all the rooms were equally warm, if not warmer, thanks to the humidity from leaking pipes. Nothing was cold, and nothing screamed "ghost".

James' information about the motel was very basic. The paperwork he had given to Shane said the ghost had been spotted there and nothing more.

The problem with tracking a ghost was that you only had so many reliable witnesses. Most of them were probably smart enough not to stick around to gather details about what they saw.

Shane covered the motel from one side to the other. Aside from broken glass, graffiti, trash, and mold, there was nothing to see. He couldn't find a single living thing, and nothing dead, either. It was as abandoned as it looked from the road.

Undeterred, Shane went around to the back of the motel, hoping to find something or at least get a new perspective. For the most part, all that existed behind the motel was a dumpster, a lot of broken furniture that had been taken out of the rooms, and then the fields of uncut grass.

Directly behind the building, however, he found a concrete patio and a swimming pool. The pool was meant to be secured behind a short chain-link fence, though the gate was torn from its hinges and anyone could now gain access.

The patio was covered in garbage, and the pool looked like a biohazard. Aside from the visible trash, the water within was almost black. Leaves, refuse, and more, floated on the surface so thick that it was hard to see below the surface.

Shane approached the pool cautiously. He knew better than to get too close to the water if there was a possibility for a ghost to be hidden there. He paced along the fence line and covered the distance slowly and purposefully. The pool was stagnant, but he could see no sign of insects or larvae in the water. It looked like the perfect breeding ground for mosquitoes, but there was no movement on or near the surface, just floating trash and clusters of clumpy, green algae.

Shane stopped and rested at the end of the fence, staring into the water. He waited for a long moment, looking from the floating garbage to the algae and back. Something stirred below the water, and the junk on the top bobbed gently. It was a gentle movement, barely creating a ripple, but it was there. Something had moved under the surface, away from sight.

Shane pulled out a cigarette and lit it. He inhaled sharply and then blew the smoke out, leaning on the fence and staring at the water.

"Going to stay down there all day?" he asked.

The water was still and silent. No answer was forthcoming. He continued to smoke as he watched the surface and waited. He was halfway through the cigarette before he sighed and moved away from the fence, taking a step toward the pool.

"You wanna do it the hard way, huh?" he said. Still no answer.

He took another step toward the edge of the pool. The trash on the surface bobbed and shifted. A hand pushed through the clusters of dead leaves and floating plastic bottles. Pale fingers spread apart as the hand reached out, looking to grab Shane's ankle now that he was in range.

Shane clutched the cigarette between his lips as he anchored himself on the edge of the pool ladder with his left hand and grabbed the ghost's wrist with his right. He was quick, not giving the ghost time to realize what was happening let alone react to it.

He pulled as hard as he could, dragging the spirit out of the water and onto the pool's edge. It slipped out of the water easily, not weighed down with water or trash since it had no corporeal form to be bothered by such things.

Shane dropped the spirit onto the ground at the side of the pool and stepped back as it rolled over, shocked and agitated to have been uprooted.

Black eyes fixed Shane with an angry stare as the spirit whipped its pale head around. The ghost was a man, perhaps in his thirties. His flesh was white and marred by large, deep-purple bruises, and he looked damp but not necessarily wet like he had died while sweating. His clothing was tattered and dirty, and the bruising across his body was extensive.

The spirit bared his teeth like an animal and hissed at Shane rather than speaking. Shane's leg was already halfway through the arc of a kick, and the ghost did not have the wherewithal to react in time. His boot hit the ghost in the chin, snapping his head back and causing him to flip over.

"I'm not interested in wasting a lot of time, so this is going to be a little uglier than usual," Shane told the ghost. He took another step toward him and kicked the spirit in the ribs. "You were stolen by people calling themselves Harvesters. There was a blonde woman, half her head shaved. What do you know about her?"

The ghost hissed again and grabbed one of Shane's ankles. He brought his other foot down on the ghost's wrist, breaking it and eliciting a new hiss, this one more frustrated than angry.

"You're going to talk eventually; it's up to you if you still have arms and legs when you do," Shane said.

The ghost's black eyes narrowed. He didn't look like he was weighing his options intelligently. Shane sighed as the ghost came at him again.

They always wanted to do things the hard way.

CHAPTER 6
BREADCRUMBS

The ghost sprang to his feet and lunged at Shane, knocking him back against the chain-link fence. The cigarette fell from his mouth, and he cursed, bringing his elbow down hard on the side of the ghost's head below the ear.

The ghost collapsed with a grunt and Shane dropped on top of him. He took the ghost's right arm and lifted it quickly, holding it by the wrist in one hand and straightening the arm with the other before snapping the elbow backward across his knee.

"Feel like talking yet?" he asked.

When the ghost did not answer, Shane twisted the arm by the wrist, still holding the biceps steady until ghostly flesh snapped and tore away. He pulled the ghost's arm off at the elbow and threw it into the pool. It barely hit the dirty surface before fading from existence, leaving the ghost with a stump.

"How about now?" he asked.

The ghost growled and struggled, and Shane took him by the other arm.

"Wait!" the ghost called out, suddenly going stiff as Shane's hand closed around his other wrist. "Just wait."

"I waited, and you didn't answer. Tell me what I need to know."

"What do you need to know?" the ghost demanded. Shane was kneeling on the spirit's gut, still holding out his good arm. It would be easy enough to break it if the ghost pushed him to do so.

"The Harvesters. What do you know about them?"

"I was in Boston," the ghost explained. "He kept me sealed up; I didn't know anything."

"Who?" Shane asked.

"Guy's name was Ennis something. Ennis Tyler? Taylor? We weren't friends," the ghost said.

The paperwork James gave Shane indicated that this ghost had been owned by a man named Ennis Tyler. He had been an infrequent client of James' and had purchased a few items over the years. This ghost had been housed in an old money clip.

"What happened?"

"No idea. He kept me in a box. It's like being trapped in your head; you can't get away from it. There's no time or space or anything. Just the dark and your thoughts. Then one day, the box is gone, and I'm here."

"What, alone? No one said anything to you?"

"There were people. The woman, the one like you said. Crazy chick with half her head shaved. She had a few people with her. They were coming after me, and I killed a couple of them. The rest of them packed up, and the woman said she'd be back one day. I never saw them again."

"Who did you kill?" Shane asked.

"How the hell should I know? I didn't ask for their ID."

"Did the woman seem disappointed? Pissed off?"

"She was… I don't know. She told one guy something about money like I ruined a job for her. That was all."

"You don't know where they went?" Shane asked.

The ghost scoffed and shook his head.

"Yeah, we exchanged addresses so we could send each other Christmas cards."

Shane grunted and, still holding the ghost's arm out with one hand, struck quickly at his elbow, breaking the arm but leaving it in one piece.

"I was telling the truth!" the ghost raged.

"Good," Shane replied. "Is that all you've got?"

"What if it is?"

"Then you've been useless and wasted my time, and I'll have to make sure you don't waste anyone else's time."

The ghost looked unsure how seriously to take the threat. The missing arm was what tipped the scales in Shane's favor.

"They didn't tell me jack, okay? But their cars had Rhode Island plates. I remember that part. Three vehicles, all Rhode Island. I remember because I hate Rhode Island. Had an ex from there."

Shane grunted and considered the ghost's words. His information had come from a few years earlier. This could have been one of Beatrix's earliest hunts. Maybe she hadn't been smart enough to rent vehicles back then. Maybe she hadn't been as serious about covering her tracks.

"Why did Ennis Tyler have you in a collection?" Shane asked.

The ghost looked confused and shook his head.

"How the hell should I know?"

Shane punched the ghost in the nose, flattening it to the right.

"Tyler had you, the woman stole you. Why? You a killer? Fighter? Soldier?"

"Man… do you not know who I am?" the ghost asked.

Shane thought it was clear that he did not. James had not included information about who the ghost was, just who had owned him before Beatrix stole him.

"I'm Eddie Bravo. Eddie Bravo, man! You know? Steady Eddie. I was a professional poker player."

Shane stared at the ghost and tried to bring something to mind. The name was vaguely familiar, but he couldn't recall how, or where he had heard it.

"You're famous?" he asked.

"Was," the ghost replied. "She even mentioned it. She called me Poker Star Dot Com, whatever the hell that means. Said I was gonna make her famous."

"Yeah, she likes nicknames," Shane said. So that was the appeal of this one. He was not a threat, he just had name recognition. The guy who paid for the hunt was probably a gambler, too. He just ended up losing.

Shane backed away from Eddie and pulled out another cigarette. He watched the ghost carefully, lighting it and considering his options.

"If you're a gambler, why the hell were you trying to drown me in a pool?"

"The last person who saw me here was your girlfriend. I didn't know what you were planning."

It was a fair enough answer. Shane shrugged and headed for the gate that led out of the pool area.

"All right, Eddie Bravo. That's all I need."

"You broke my arm, man! You ripped off the other one! What the hell am I supposed to do like this?"

"How should I know? Take up soccer? I don't know."

The ghost struggled to his feet as Shane began to walk away.

"You can't leave me here like this!"

"You're free to leave. Besides, the blonde still knows you're here, and she'll finish the job if she ever comes back. You better hope I find her first."

"Come on. That's not fair. I told you everything I know!"

"Good to know," Shane said.

He left, ignoring the ghost ranting behind him, and returned to the front of the motel where he'd left his car. James' list had more names on it. It wasn't a trail, and certainly no sort of straight line, but it was something.

If he could get bits and pieces of information from all the ghosts he encountered, he might be able to paint a picture of who Beatrix was and, more importantly, where she was. So far, Rhode Island seemed like a good lead. The state was small, and he needed to make it smaller.

The closest lead to Greenfield that James had provided Shane was a small town a few miles out of Boston called Swampscott. Shane had never been there, but he suspected it was a real blink-and-you'll-miss-it place.

The drive took a couple of hours, and he stopped along the way to get another coffee and something quick to eat. When he got to Swampscott, he realized the town was bigger than he had expected. That wasn't saying much, but the place had a population of over ten thousand, and he had anticipated four corners and maybe a church.

The address James provided was out of date. Not only because the family of the one-time client no longer lived there, but it was also that the house was gone. There was an empty plot of land at the address, a plowed-under lot primed for new construction. At that moment, it was full of weeds and grass.

The land looked well-settled, and it had been some years since the house had vanished. Shane drove slowly and pulled over three houses down when he saw a man out front watering his lawn.

"Hey there. You live here long?" Shane asked, approaching the man. The houses in the neighborhood looked to date back to the seventies. The man dated back even earlier. He was lanky and tall with a noticeable sway in his back. Shane guessed he was just past retirement age.

"Who's asking?" the man said, keeping the hose running.

"I got an address from my old man's things. Friend of his used to live at fifty-seven Rothway, and I'm looking at an empty lot where fifty-seven should be. Wondering if you know what happened."

"Friend of your father's?" the man asked.

"Yeah. He passed away recently and had something he wanted to give to what I guess was an old friend, but… I don't know what to do now."

The man grimaced and shut off the hose.

"I'm sorry to be the one to tell you, but the family who used to live there all passed away years ago. Real tragedy, too. Three of them died the same night. Home invasion robbery, the police said."

"Oh, wow," Shane said, trying to sound suitably shocked. "When did that happen?"

"Must be six years ago now? Maybe more. The bank took possession of the place, but they couldn't sell it after what happened. Eventually, they tore it down. Keep hearing maybe someone is buying the land, but as you can see, there's nothing yet."

Shane nodded, looking back down the road at the empty lot. That threw a wrench into his plans. If the house had been torn down, the ghost could have been removed along with it. He wasn't sure when James' information on a ghost sighting had last been updated.

"Have you noticed anything unusual in the neighborhood since the house was torn down?" Shane asked.

The man raised an eyebrow and started up the hose again.

"Unusual in what way?" he asked.

Shane shrugged.

"Anything you can't explain."

"Aside from these new smartphones and thermostats that talk to you, and DNA tests for dogs, and that sort of thing?" the man asked.

Shane nodded and took a step back toward the road.

"No, I suppose not. Thanks for your time," he said.

The older man nodded and returned to watering the lawn. If Beatrix had let a ghost loose after killing the man who once owned it, and his family, it probably had learned better than to expose itself in the neighborhood. Most likely, it was keeping to itself as well as it could.

The motel had been an easy location to track a ghost. A residential neighborhood was another matter. Shane would have to be a lot more observant—and careful—if he wanted to track this one.

CHAPTER 7

DON'T GO IN THE FOREST

Shane walked the neighborhood, circling the block and observing what he could from the sidewalk. He passed a handful of pedestrians, but no one paid him any mind.

Nothing in the neighborhood looked out of place, and if there was a ghost haunting any of the houses, it hadn't disturbed anyone else in the area enough to make it obvious. Nothing reminded him of his home on Berkley Street. Nothing seemed ominous. There were no places where the birds refused to fly or where even insects seemed scarce. It looked like any average, forgettable neighborhood that Shane had seen a thousand times over.

He circled the block and was ready to head down the street to the next neighborhood when something got his attention. The opposite side of the street was only a single row of houses, behind which was open land, and, in the distance, a small, wooded area. At the end of that street, on the corner just ahead of Shane, was a ghost.

The spirit sat under a tree with his feet over the curb. He looked like he was waiting for a ride from someone. The ghost was that of a young man, probably only midway through his teens, Shane decided as he got closer. His face was covered in freckles, and his curly red hair was matted with blood from a wound on the side of his head. He had clearly died in some kind of accident.

Shane crossed the street and the ghost didn't even lift his head. The spirit seemed preoccupied with looking at his feet though there was nothing interesting to see. He wore an old pair of Converse tennis shoes with the white star on the side.

"Those shoes don't seem that fascinating," Shane said, stopping under the tree.

"They cost me fourteen dollars brand-new," the ghost said. He didn't look up, surprising Shane with his indifference.

"Set you back about eighty bucks today," Shane pointed out.

"Good thing I got them when I did, I guess," the boy replied. "Mowed twenty lawns to get the money. Got a Coke and some fries at the mall at the same time. It was a good day."

The ghost still had not even looked at Shane. His demeanor was not what Shane expected. This was not the ghost Shane was looking for.

"You been in this neighborhood long?"

"Why you asking?" the ghost replied.

Finally, he lifted his head, squinting up at Shane as though the sun was in his eyes.

"I'm looking for someone who went missing a few years ago."

"Call the police," the ghost said, looking down again.

Shane chuckled and pulled out a cigarette, lighting it while he watched the young man watching his shoes.

"I'm looking for a ghost."

"Yeah, well, we don't have a club or anything," the boy replied.

"You're not surprised I can see you. Had run-ins with people who can see you in the past?"

"Once or twice," the ghost admitted. "Doesn't matter. They almost always freak out."

"What about the ones who don't?"

The ghost looked at him again, taking in everything from Shane's boots up to his face.

"What are you, some kind of soldier?"

"I was," Shane said.

"My stepdad had boots like that," he said, pointing to Shane's. "Wore them all the time, even after they kicked him out."

"They're comfortable," Shane admitted.

"Not when someone's kicking your skull in with them."

Shane exhaled slowly and nodded as the boy returned to looking at his feet.

"No, I imagine they wouldn't be," he said.

A long silence passed. Shane smoked and watched the ghost until the boy finally looked at him again.

"So, who are you looking for?"

"There used to be a house, next block over. Got torn down, but a friend told me a ghost used to be in that house. It was let loose after the people there died."

The ghost was frowning now.

"Who are you?"

"Guy who needs to find out where that ghost is and who set him loose," he replied.

"The people who did it saw me. It was a man and a woman. She saw me. She was bleeding, and she gave me the finger guns, you know?"

The ghost raised his hand, pointing at Shane and then flexing his thumb the way a child does when pretending to shoot.

"Yeah. She say anything? Why was she bleeding?"

"She said, 'Watch your back, Freckles,' and then pretended to shoot me twice. She was bleeding because someone shot her, I think."

"Blonde. Half-shaved head?" Shane asked.

The boy pursed his lips and shook his head.

"Buzzcut all over," he answered. "Looked mean in a weird way. Laughed a lot."

"Yeah. Yeah, that's who I need to find. What happened to the ghost?"

The young man shook his head again and returned his focus to his feet.

"You don't want to find that one."

"I do," Shane said. "If I want to find that woman and stop her from killing people like she killed that family, I need to find the ghost."

"He's not… good, you know? The ghost, I mean. I don't know why that family had him in their house. I never saw him before they died. I don't know what set him off, or how this woman you're looking for let him loose in the world, but he's not good. It's not safe to be near him."

The ghost's tone was very serious, but his voice was low. He picked at the star symbol on his shoe and seemed to be going out of his way to avoid looking at Shane while he spoke.

"What do you mean?" Shane asked.

"When he left that house, I think he wanted to be free. He could have gone into another house; there are lots of places around. But he didn't. He went into the woods. And ever since then, every once in a while, someone goes in there and never comes out again."

"He's been killing people?"

"I don't go in there. I don't know what he does with them. I'm not stupid; I know they're not alive anymore. The police come sometimes and look around. They never find anything. They don't find tracks, they don't find clothes, and they sure don't find bodies. They don't find anything. No one ever does. He makes sure of it."

"How many people have gone missing?" Shane asked.

"Maybe a dozen that I know about. Maybe more. Like I said, I don't go in there. He saw me, too. When he first left the house after the people died, he saw me first. He smiled at me, and I never wanted to see his face again."

"No one knows it's this thing in the woods that's taking people?"

"Why would they?" the ghost replied. "He's a ghost. No one sees him. He doesn't leave a trail. They might as well be going to the moon."

Shane nodded and exhaled a puff of smoke. The trail to connect the dots from the house and the family that had died to the disappearances in the woods was not one that a regular living person was likely to see. It sounded like no one knew the ghost was in the house to begin with, aside from James Moran and Beatrix. And whoever gave Beatrix her information.

Either someone was stealing information from James' files, or the owners of these ghosts were too trusting with someone else in their community. Shane knew that James dealt with a lot of the same people regularly. He had an exclusive clientele, usually people who were well off, and who were into the extremely rare hobby of collecting haunted items.

Shane was familiar with these people because he was familiar with James. He had also had run-ins with the Cult of the Endless Night and other groups in which members were living people who collected ghosts. There had to be something like that linking these people to the Harvesters.

The problem was this wasn't like being a member of the local 4-H club. This wasn't just an exclusive club. This was something no sane person would discuss in public. You don't just tell your coworkers you collect homicidal spirits for kicks.

When most of the world didn't believe in ghosts and would assume you were mentally ill for entertaining the idea, you had to choose who you associated with in this world. Secrecy layered in secrecy was the order of the day. Shane was learning that finding out who Beatrix got her marching orders from was a dangerous and laborious task.

James Moran had seemed like Shane's best bet for getting a break, but he had come up with little so far. He might have just been looking in the wrong places. It wasn't as though everyone shared their life story with James when they bought an item from him. The first ghost, Cassius, hadn't even come from James. Shane and the others were overlooking something, or they just hadn't encountered it yet.

"Where is the best place to go if I want to talk to this ghost?" Shane asked.

The ghost on the curb looked up at him again and laughed mockingly.

"You can just walk in front of a car if you wanna die that badly," he answered.

"Humor me," Shane said.

The ghost sighed and got to his feet, brushing off his pants as though they might have dirt on them. He started walking away from his tree and down the street past the single row of houses.

"I'm not gonna go in with you," the ghost warned.

"Fair enough," Shane replied. "I just need a general direction."

"He's gonna kill you."

"Let me worry about that."

The ghost led Shane to the edge of the woods where the trees met the open patch of land behind the houses and stopped.

"See that?" he said, pointing to a footpath worn into the dirt that led into the forest.

"That leads to him?"

"That leads into the woods. I don't know where he is in there, and I don't want to. But I've seen people walk down that path and never come back out."

"Good enough," Shane said. "Thanks."

He left the road and took the path across a small expanse of grass and then into the forest.

"Hey, are these really worth eighty bucks now?" the ghost asked, gesturing to his shoes.

"Brand-new. Those are vintage. Probably worth a lot more," Shane replied.

The ghost smiled and nodded appreciatively. He stayed on the road and watched as Shane entered the woods, on a worn footpath through the trees and into the tight, cluttered space beyond.

CHAPTER 8
NATURE'S WRATH

The forest had ferns and wildflowers and other kinds of growth that threatened to obscure the path Shane walked on. He navigated past several fallen and mostly rotten trees, and across a shallow stream that was home to an abundance of small frogs vocally expressing their disgust at Shane's passing.

He'd walked along the meandering path for close to twenty minutes when he noticed the landscape beginning to change. The lush greenery became sparser. The plants that were growing were darker, lower to the ground, and less lush.

Where birds in the trees had been common when he entered, the symphony of forest life had slowly quieted. He heard birds in the distance behind him now, but nothing waited ahead. It was as though the woods were dying around him. He was on the right track.

The path became clear as the size of the plants obscuring it shrank. They grew farther and farther apart until most of the forest floor was dried leaves and old, brown pine needles with only the faintest bits of greenery poking out here and there.

Jumbles of dead branches and tree limbs lay about, the remnants of some storm in the past that had torn apart the canopy and left skeletal fragments tossed around haphazardly. The path was clear, though barely wide enough to allow Shane to stand with his feet together.

He continued forward, well beyond where he entered, and so deep, he could no longer hear even faint sounds from the town. As the underbrush thinned out even more, the sounds of the distant birds began to fade as well, and soon, he was in silence, save for the sound of leaves crushing beneath his boots as he walked.

The trees were thinner than they were where Shane entered. The trunks were wizened and, in many cases, crooked and bent. The number of dead trees began to outnumber the living. They were gray, dry hulks with curved, sinewy branches devoid of leaves and covered in flaking bark.

Ahead, through the thinning tree cover, Shane saw a shape. It was a hulk of something, a pile of wood and leaves at first glance, but the closer he got, the clearer it became that this was not a natural pile of deadfall. It was massive and resembled a beaver dam without the water. Branches, logs, and even whole fallen trees seemed pulled together with a purpose. Someone had created a mound of dead things jumbled together like some funerary mound in the middle of nowhere.

Shane approached slowly, looking for any signs of movement. He was within twenty yards of the mound of forest refuse when he heard a twig snap. He turned and scanned the sparse tree cover but saw nothing.

Rather than moving forward, Shane stopped. With the mound still in sight, he lit a new cigarette and leaned against one of the dead trees. The ghost would have seen him by now. He would wait for the ghost to come to him rather than the other way around.

The minutes ticked by, and Shane stayed where he was, comfortable and relaxed against the tree. He smoked in silence and waited. As the sun passed in the sky, the shadows of the trees grew longer, stretching beyond him like monstrous arms reaching for the mound he had discovered.

The dry, crunchy sound of leaves broke through the silence of the still forest. Shane turned toward the noise, somewhere behind him, and was not surprised to see empty forest and nothing more.

The sound was a footstep. One clear, precise step into dry leaves. It was intentional. Shane did nothing about it. Instead, he finished his cigarette, fieldstripping it and slipping it back into the pack when he was done.

Another twig snapped, this time on Shane's left. He turned to see if anything was there and only caught the barest flash of movement on his right. Before he knew what was happening, his feet were pulled out from under him with a swift and decisive jerk. He fell backward, his head hitting the ground and causing a wave of pain to radiate through his body as his skull seemed to explode.

His ankle was still gripped tightly as the ghost pulled him toward the mound of dead branches and logs. Shane struggled to sit up and saw that it was not a ghost pulling him but a tangle of thin, brown vines that had ensnared him.

Shane tried to lean forward far enough to grab at the vine and pull it loose or cut it, but it jerked harshly, pulling him backward. By the time he lifted his head again, he was being pulled through an opening in the mound of deadfall, a ramshackle doorway low to the ground.

He was dragged across uneven ground, with shards of broken wood and rock biting into his flesh as he was pulled deeper and deeper into the darkness. The deadfall was piled so thickly that almost no light got inside. Only the faintest hints broke through here and there, just enough to ensure he wasn't in pitch blackness. Shane was certain that was intentional as well, as the ghost would want its prey to see what was happening.

The vine let loose and whipped away into the darkness, depositing Shane in a chamber inside the deadfall hovel. It was a wide room but not quite tall enough to stand in. The floor was muddy and had been cleared away of most of the debris, leaving only bare earth. A bubbling pool of water gurgled and churned in the middle like a spring.

Dead things lined the room, most of them pushed to the edges. Much of what Shane saw had been reduced to bone. Some were animals. He saw the skulls of what might have been raccoons or skunks. But there were more human remains. Hands, ribs, and skulls were tossed here and there, the way someone might discard food wrappers.

On the far side of the bubbling spring, the largest pile of bones was stacked in mimicry of the deadfall hovel. Shane picked out several human bones, but there were also smaller ones to give the pile more girth and density.

Shane got to his feet, hunched over in the small space. As he did so, the ghost rose to meet him, climbing out of the pile of bones. He was surprised to see that the spirit was slight of build, no more than five feet tall, and able to stand upright in the enclosed space. He was not remarkably thin but certainly not fat or muscular. His flesh was pale and waxy, and he was nude save for a pair of plain, black dress shoes.

The ghost's body glistened with a strange sheen like oily sweat. His hair was cut short and plain. While his overall physical presence was not intimidating, and he would have been unremarkable as a living man, something was genuinely unpleasant about his face.

He was not deformed. He had not suffered great trauma that left him scarred or mutilated the way some spirits had. He wasn't even especially ugly. Not in a way that would be memorable or noteworthy. Instead, he was simply unpleasant to look at.

The ghost regarded Shane with wide eyes. They were too wide, too intense, and unblinking. His nostrils seemed permanently flared, and the curve of his mouth gave it the look of forever holding a lascivious smile. It made the ghost look like it was thinking unpleasant thoughts. There was something vulgar about the expression, and Shane found himself grimacing at the sight.

"More meat for me," the ghost said. His voice was soft and quiet. It matched his expression perfectly, being both unpleasant and seeming to insinuate something even worse than the spoken word just by the tone. Shane was immediately disgusted.

The ghost came for him, walking forward slowly out of the pile of bones. He moved shamelessly, not embarrassed by how exposed he was and in no way fearful that Shane could harm him.

"You've killed a lot of people here," Shane said, looking around the space.

"The sweetest treats," the ghost replied breathily. He reached for Shane with small, thin-fingered hands.

Shane caught the ghost's wrist. The wide-eyed, unsettling glare quickly became an expression of shock, but Shane gave it no time to react. Instead, he forced the ghost forward as he bent and pulled back his arm. The ghost stumbled and jerked about easily, so surprised by Shane's attack that he hadn't resisted until it was too late.

With his arm twisted behind his back, the ghost fell forward with a kick from Shane against the back of his legs. Shane forced him face-down into the mud next to the pool and twisted the arm as sharply as possible. The ghost's shoulder popped out of its socket, and he gasped into the thick, sodden earth.

"I need to ask you some questions," Shane said. He twisted again and pulled. The slick, pale flesh of the ghost's shoulder tore and the arm separated. Shane tossed it aside.

"Nooooo," the ghost whined, sputtering in the mud. "I never hurt you. It's not fair."

The ghost's voice had taken on an insolent, childlike quality. It was still breathy but had a higher pitch that Shane found very aggravating.

"Focus," he said, ignoring the complaints. "Tell me about the Harvesters."

"It's not fair," the ghost whined again, writhing about like a fish beneath Shane.

He knelt in the small of the slight man's back and pivoted to face his legs. The ghost was kicking, like having a tantrum, and Shane caught one of the legs. He broke the ankle and then snapped the foot to the left, tearing it off as he had done with the arm. The appendage faded from existence as it dropped from Shane's grip.

"You only have so many parts to lose. Consider that before choosing your next words. Tell me about the Harvesters," Shane ordered.

"I don't know Harvesters. I don't know what that means. Please let me up. I'll be good to you, I promise. I'll be a good friend."

The tone of the ghost's voice was still repugnant, and Shane twisted the already wounded leg. The ghost responded with a sound reminiscent of an injured animal.

"I spoke true!" the spirit whined.

"The people who freed you. A man and a woman. What do you know about them?"

"What freedom? I'm free, I'm always free," the ghost said.

Shane snapped the leg at the knee, bending it fully back in the wrong direction.

"It comes off next time," he said.

"The woman! The shaved woman. Yes, I know that woman. She came to the house and asked me to come play. Not free, just to play. I know her. I do," the ghost replied. "Don't hurt me again. I'm your friend! We can be friends!"

"Tell me about Beatrix," Shane said.

"Beatrix? No, friend. That's not her name. Brandy. Brandy Jean. Do you know Brandy Jean?" the ghost asked.

Shane grunted.

"Shaved head? Can talk to ghosts? Hurt them?"

"Yes, dear Brandy Jean. That's her. I knew her long ago. She's a friend, like you. We can all be friends!"

Shane turned back to the ghost's head and grabbed him by the hair, lifting his face from the mud.

"What do you mean long ago?"

"Before this place. I knew her when she was just a wee, precious thing. Oh, such a precocious child she was."

"Where?" Shane asked.

"Rhode Island! In the house on the beach. It was lovely there in the storms. When the waves came raging and no one could hear a sound.

Deep, down inside. Not even a scream."

James Moran had told Shane that this ghost came from the people who lived in the house that had been destroyed. He was in their collection, and Beatrix came after him. But if the sniveling, unpleasant thing Shane was crushing into the mud spoke the truth, she knew of the ghost long before then.

"Tell me about it. How did you know her? And how did you end up here?"

"I told you. I speak the truth, friend. I promise. It was in the house on the beach. Sweet little Brandy Jean came. She destroyed another ghost there. I saw her do it, just like you. I saw her pull his head from his shoulders, and the most glorious warmth came from his body as it fell apart. It bathed me like the light of the moon."

"Less poetry," Shane said.

"Yes! I'll tell you everything; I swear it," the ghost said, grinning his unwholesome grin.

CHAPTER 9

THE DEATH OF BRANDY JEAN

"Why didn't she destroy you, too?" Shane asked.

"I hid. I knew that we couldn't play because of the Shadow. Not yet. Too dangerous to play with Brandy Jean back then."

"She didn't track you? Didn't have machines that could see you hiding?"

"Machines?" the ghost said with a childish giggle. "No machines can see me. She couldn't see me."

What the ghost was talking about must have preceded Beatrix being part of the Harvesters. Before they had the technology to hunt spirits. If she had a different name back then, it could have been the beginning of her ghost hunting days. She caught one, but this thing got away from her. At least for a while.

"So, she left you. How did you get here?"

"Someone else found me. Sneaky little trickster, that one. Didn't look for me, looked for my special secret. He put me away somewhere, and when I came free again, I was here. I was in the house, and then, soon, Brandy Jean, all grown up, came to play again. But I sneaked away, just like before. She said she'd come back one day, but nothing so far. Just you! Just my new friend."

"How old was Brandy Jean in Rhode Island?" Shane asked.

"Oh, sweet little Brandy Jean. Just a girl then. Just a child, she was."

"How old?" Shane asked.

"Seventeen, maybe? I never asked to see her ID."

The ghost laughed and Shane pushed his face back into the mud, cutting him off. That could very well have been Beatrix's first foray into hunting ghosts. Like Shane, she would have known earlier that she could see them; she might have even had to fight for her life against some. But at some point, when she was still young, she started actively going after them.

Somewhere along the line, she decided to change her name. She dropped Brandy Jean and became Beatrix. She hooked up with Lanthimos, Kraft, Tully, and whoever else was in her squad. They made contact with someone who could be the brains of the operation, and probably the bankroll, too. Someone who could afford to get them toys that could stun spirits and track them by their heat signature.

"Where was the house in Rhode Island?" Shane asked, pulling the ghost's head up again.

"The beach! Beautiful view of the ocean. We can go there, you and I. Just us. You'll love it. I know you will."

Shane grunted. Useless information from a disturbed ghost would not get him far.

"What happened here? The house with the family that died, where Brandy Jean found you again."

The ghost hummed and smiled.

"It was all so very exciting. I had been hidden away for so long, and then suddenly, there I was. Sweet Brandy Jean was so much older, and there was a man, his wife, and their precious little girl. The man shot Brandy Jean, and everyone screamed, and it was such a beautiful sound after so long. I wanted more, and so I took it from them. I took all the screams they had."

"*You* killed the family," Shane said.

"It was just three of them," the ghost said, as though that somehow made a difference. "Brandy Jean came for me, and I ran away. She chased me, but her wound was so grievous that she had to quit. She told me I wasn't free just yet. She threw my special secret thing into these woods and

63

promised she'd be back."

The answers weren't as in-depth as Shane had hoped, but had more confirmation that Rhode Island was where he had to go. And that the reason they had so much trouble finding Beatrix was that she was using a fake name. Brandy Jean with no last name was very little to go on, but it was something. She had been covering her tracks for years, but Shane was slowly uncovering them.

"You see, friend? I'm true to my word. I helped. Didn't I help?" the ghost asked.

Shane looked around. The ghost of the boy said around a dozen people had gone missing in the woods. Shane guessed there were at least that many bodies in the room with him, probably more.

"Who were all these people?" Shane asked, gesturing to the bones.

"Gifts," the ghost said in his breathy voice, sounding excited. "Gifts of the forest. They come to me now and then. They wander right up to my door. They want me to take them. They want me to peel away all that tender, soft meat. Such a gift from all my friends."

Shane adjusted his position on the ghost's back, shifting from one knee to the other as he knelt on his spine. The ghost was still squirming, but not nearly as strongly as he had been.

"I helped. Didn't I help my new friend?" the ghost asked.

"You sure did," Shane said. "Very helpful."

Shane took the ghost's head in his hands and squeezed. The spirit giggled at first and then, as the bones of his skull collapsed, he began squealing like a wild pig caught in a trap. The sound lasted only a moment. Shane's hands came together, and the skull was crushed.

The cold body of the ghost exploded and knocked Shane backward into the pile of bones beyond the bubbling spring. They scattered under his weight, and the hovel listed hard to the left but stayed upright.

Shane was forced to crawl out of the tunnel through which he'd been dragged to begin with. He moved swiftly on his knees and elbows until he was outside and able to stand upright in the light of the sun again.

Rhode Island was where he needed to go, but he still needed more directions. Looking for a random house on the beach where somebody might know the name Beatrix or Brandy Jean was not going to be easy.

Shane wondered when Beatrix had killed off Brandy Jean. That had to be her real name if the ghost was correct about how old she had been. She was still a teen back then, but she knew what she could do, and she exercised that power. If she was destroying spirits that young, she had probably endured experiences not dissimilar from those Shane had gone through as a child.

While Shane had chosen a path that took him to the Marines, something had pushed Beatrix toward the hunt. Maybe it was the benefactor about which he still knew so little.

Free from the ghost's hideaway, Shane's phone sounded a notification. He pulled it from his pocket and saw a message from Agent Ventura.

Got a hit on Lanthimos. Old, but it's all I have for now. Last known address. Could be worth a look.

Shane checked the attachment that came with the message. It was a limited file, but it listed an address for Adrian Lanthimos in a place called Fall River, Massachusetts. Another small town Shane had never been to, but it was right on the border between Massachusetts and Rhode Island.

The address was all the confirmation Shane needed that he was on the right track. The answers would be in Rhode Island, he just needed to ask the right questions to narrow it down. Maybe Lanthimos would have some more pieces to the puzzle.

He returned to his car and left Swampscott, heading down to Fall River. The drive was another hour and a half, and it was late afternoon by the time he arrived.

Fall River was another city that was much larger than Shane had anticipated. Tracking down the address Ventura had given him took longer than he expected. The city was located on a bay, and a massive bridge across the water was visible before he even got into the town.

Shane made his way to Central Street, the address Ventura had provided, and drove slowly until he came to what looked like an abandoned storefront. The building looked like it had been condemned some years earlier, the front was boarded up and covered in graffiti, and the windows on the upper floors were covered with newspaper on the inside.

The neighborhood around it looked a little rundown. The stonework was crumbling around the buildings that were still in use, and the address Shane had for Lanthimos was the worst of the lot.

There was evidence that a sign had once been on the front wall, with the stain of the removed letters like a stencil. The building had once been home to something called Landon's Pharmacy. The two floors above looked like apartments, however, and the only door Shane saw was in the corner of the building, boarded up, and sealed tight.

Shane drove around the block to get a feel for what he was dealing with. The rest of the neighborhood was quiet and not as ramshackle as the abandoned pharmacy, but not lively, either. It looked like one of those tired ends of town that people had abandoned over the years, desperately in need of a revival or a bulldozer.

He parked a block away from the derelict building and walked back toward it, observing as much as he could of the surrounding area as he did so. Traffic was light, and there were no shops or other points of interest, just a handful of old homes in need of upkeep.

A sign was posted on the entrance at the corner of the building where the door once faced the street before it was boarded up. The city had condemned the building some years earlier, and it was scheduled to be torn down. The posted demolition date had long since passed, which made

Shane wonder just how slow things worked in Fall River.

Shane circled the building in search of an access point. Whoever had boarded it up had done a good job. All possible entrances looked well-sealed.

The rear of the building had a second door that overlooked a footpath that ran down the street between the backs of the buildings and a small bit of green space on a hill that led to another street. This second boarded-up door was recessed into an alcove. Shane guessed it was the entrance to the living spaces above the pharmacy.

He looked around and couldn't see anyone. As casually as he could, he slammed his foot into the first plank of wood covering the doorway. It snapped easily and broke a pane of glass behind it.

After another quick look around, Shane pulled the plank out of his way and used his elbow to clear glass from the door. He reached through the hole he'd broken and unlocked the door from the inside. It pushed in, leaving the rest of the wooden planks nailed in place across the open doorframe.

He pulled several out of the way until he had enough room to slip through, and then hastily moved the planks back in place so that they at least looked like they were covering the spot. Anyone passing by probably wouldn't have noticed things were amiss unless they got too close.

Shane found himself in a small lobby. The place smelled musty, and there were six mailboxes set into the wall with smudged, illegible labels attached to them. A narrow flight of stairs led to a door on the second floor, and there was nothing else in the space beyond the dusty, old tiles.

He took the stairs to the door and found it wedged shut. It took several hard shoves with his shoulder to get the door to open into a long, empty hallway with doors on either side.

Someone had pulled the light fixtures from the ceiling, stripping away the wires, and leaving them empty. Other wires had been pulled from the walls, leaving strips of shattered drywall and chunks of material on the ugly, stained carpet that extended from the doorway to a boarded-up window at the far end.

There was a smell in the place that Shane couldn't identify. Some of it was the musty smell of age, but there was something else there, like old food or maybe the smell of a dumpster after it had been emptied. It smelled sour but forgotten, like he had missed the worst of it by a few years.

Shane had been around enough dead things to realize what he smelled. The city of Fall River might have condemned the building and scheduled it for demolition, but someone hadn't cleaned it out thoroughly.

Something dead was waiting for him.

CHAPTER 10

WHERE ROTTEN THINGS WAIT

Shane tried the first door on his left. The cheap brass "one" was still screwed to the door, though it was spotted with corrosion. The door was unlocked but still took an effort to open, as it was warped in its frame and stuck on the floorboards. Shane had to kick it just below the doorknob to get it to budge.

The interior of the apartment was a relic of the sixties or seventies. It wasn't spacious, but it wasn't the most cramped place Shane had seen. It was ugly. Rust-orange and olive-green wallpaper were offset by tile the color of urine in the tiny kitchen. The rest of the apartment was finished in green carpet that matched the wallpaper and looked like pea-soup vomit.

Someone had ransacked the flat just as they had done to the hallway outside. There were holes in the walls where copper wire had been stripped away. Everything that could have been stolen was gone. The faucets were missing, the handles for the kitchen drawers and cupboards were missing, and even the curtain rods were gone.

Aside from the rubble of broken walls, there wasn't anything left in the apartment indicating who might have stayed there or what they did while they were there. Shane left quickly and crossed the hall to apartment two.

The second apartment had only been half-stripped. The wires were gone, but someone had left behind the handles for the kitchen cupboards. The wallpaper and the carpet were identical. Clearly, whoever owned the building had not put much effort into decorating. There was more garbage in this apartment, evidence that people had been there some years ago.

Shane saw beer cans that hadn't been sold in more than ten years, and a crushed pizza box with a nearly petrified crust inside.

Nothing in the apartment indicated who had lived there or that anything related to Beatrix or the Harvesters was linked to it. Shane left the place quickly and returned to the hall.

The smell in the building grew stronger as he approached the third apartment. There were moldy undertones now, the sense of something damp waiting behind one of the doors. The sour, rotten odor was more pronounced.

The door to three was locked, and Shane was forced to break it down. It took several kicks using his whole weight to gain access.

Plastic sheeting gave way as the door pushed in. Someone had hung strips of thick plastic above the inner door frame. The reason became apparent as soon as Shane was inside. The plastic was to help seal in the stench.

This apartment was more humid than the others, and the smell was fetid and rotten. The door opened into the kitchen, with the rest of the apartment to the right. The kitchen featured scattered bits of refuse including some old cans, a broken coffee mug, and a few scattered utensils.

Mold was prevalent along the walls, which were still intact and had not had the wires stripped from them. Shane opened one of the kitchen drawers and found it cluttered with Chinese takeout menus, batteries, a pack of matches, and junk mail.

"Adrianos Lanthimos," Shane read aloud, holding up a letter from a credit card company. He was in the right place. He picked through the rest of the mail but found nothing of interest.

Shane left the kitchen and ventured deeper into the apartment. There was still a sofa and a broken coffee table in the living room. Indentations in the carpet showed where a chair had once been, but there were just scattered bits of garbage now. Shane saw labels from beer bottles, what looked like fingernail clippings, and plenty of food crumbs. Nothing to give insight into who Lanthimos was, or what he did.

The smell was rank, something damp mixed with something rotten. He passed through the living room into the small hallway that led to a single bedroom and a bathroom. Both doors were closed, but the carpet in the hallway was squishy and sodden, or maybe it was the floor beneath the carpet. In any event, things felt soft and pliant in a way that made him uncomfortable.

Shane opened the door to the bathroom and took a step back, wincing and covering his face. The floor of the bathroom was covered in a layer of damp, black sludge. The bathtub was full to the brim with something dark and thick. The curtains in the room were closed, so there was not enough light to make out what he was seeing. He had no desire to venture in and pull the curtains back.

The room smelled like a stagnant pond, a summer smell of rotten fish and sewage that built up in a pool full of dead things and scummy vegetation. The humidity was so thick, he felt it on his face like a coating of slime. He closed the door quickly and turned toward the bedroom.

The floor squished as he walked the three paces from the bathroom. He adjusted his footing so that he was closer to the walls, where the floorboards felt sturdier and more supportive.

The bedroom door took some effort to open. The wood was warped in the frame and didn't want to cooperate. Shane slammed into it several times until it fell open.

This room was the source of the sour, dead smell that lingered behind everything else. Shane was glad to have gotten there as late as he did because he was certain the stench would have been unbearable if he had arrived when it was still festering.

Late afternoon sunlight streamed through the uncovered window, lighting a bed in the center of the room. The bare mattress was devoid of sheets and stained brown around the corpse that lay upon it.

Shane guessed the body had been there for years. There was not much left to it, though it had not yet been reduced to bones. Flesh like jerky was still attached to the skeleton, stretched across the skull, ribs, arms, and legs. All of it looked dry now, save for an oily sheen.

The body clearly wasn't Lanthimos, but there was no way to tell who it might have been. The decay was so bad that Shane couldn't even guess the sex.

The room looked ransacked, or at least someone had packed up very hastily. The sliding door to the closet was pulled off, and drawers in a dresser were left open. Articles of clothing and old papers were scattered about. The ones on the floor had gone moldy long ago, but items on the dresser, piled on a chair, and heaped in the corner fared a little better.

The floor sagged under his feet as he approached the nightstand next to the bed. He rifled through the top drawer, looking for anything that might explain more about who Beatrix's sidekick was.

Cool air tickled the back of Shane's head, and he turned around quickly. A figure stood in the open closet doorway, staring out at him with sunken eyes. The ghost had more flesh than the corpse on the mattress, but it was easy to see they were one and the same. The spirit looked emaciated, with only the beginning days of decay affecting it.

"I don't suppose you know Adrian Lanthimos," Shane said.

The skin on the ghost's face was saggy, and it moved independently of the skull underneath it like it was wearing a loose mask. The conditions had caused it to decay in a way that stained it brownish green. Even the eyes were off, the whites now a dark yellow.

The ghost spoke to Shane in a language he didn't recognize. It sounded almost Greek, but none of the words were familiar. While the content of its speech was unknown, the emotion behind it was a little easier to figure out. The ghost was angry that Shane was there.

"Just here to find out about Lanthimos, that's all," Shane said.

The ghost growled and let loose a string of words Shane couldn't understand but didn't need to. There was a threat in there, the tone was unmistakable. It shambled forward then, coming for Shane with a hateful sneer on its loose, hanging, rotted lips.

Shane met the ghost at the side of the bed, catching its hands as it reached for him. The defense startled the ghost, but it adapted quickly, kicking Shane in the thigh and pressing onward, causing him to fall back.

They landed on the bed, Shane hitting the corpse and the ghost landing on top of him. Shane held fast to the spirit's rotten wrists, but the ghost had switched tactics and was now biting at Shane's face.

Shane pushed up on the ghost's wrists, forcing the torso up. He then raised a leg, planting his foot in the ghost's stomach and kicking it off. He rolled off the corpse and to the side of the bed, getting back to his feet on the squishy carpet just as the ghost lunged again.

It hit Shane hard in the gut, wrapping its arms around him and digging sharp claws into his back as it dragged him to the ground. Shane fell hard next to the bed, and an ominous creak from the wood preceded the floor buckling underneath them.

The rotten carpet split and Shane fell through to the floor below, landing hard on a pile of discarded shelves in the pharmacy. He cried out in pain as metal edges dug into his spine and lower back.

The ghost fell with Shane and was still on top of him when the shelves broke their fall. He struggled to right himself, but the ghost began its attack once more, grasping at Shane's throat with its cold hands and squeezing as though it meant to pop his head from his shoulders.

Shane took hold of one of the ghost's wrists in both of his hands and applied pressure. He pushed up with his left hand and twisted with his right, breaking the nearly skeletal wrist with a dry snap.

The ghost's jaundiced eyes stared into his as it raged in another language. Shane ignored it, looking past the ghost at the ceiling above his head. The rot from the bedroom had spread throughout the pharmacy ceiling and stained it black. Shane saw the floor still buckling above just as the bed collapsed through it.

He rolled quickly to one side, tearing the ghost's hand from its wrist. The bed from Lanthimos' apartment crashed onto the shelves where Shane had been a moment earlier and continued down.

The pharmacy floor buckled and caved in. Shane found himself falling for a second time, following the bed through a second hole into the building's basement. Shelves, floor tiles, and pounds of debris collapsed into the hole alongside Shane, raining on him as he hit the cement floor.

Shane landed face-down on the cold, wet ground. He groaned as he got to his hands and knees, looking around to orient himself. The pharmacy had been dark, with the only light coming through cracks in the boarded-up windows. In the basement, the faintest light cascaded down through the hole, illuminating the broken bed and the damaged corpse on top of it, and little else.

Shane looked around but saw no sign of the ghost. The basement was submerged in about an inch of water. There were rotten old boxes, more shelves, and bags of trash piled all over. Too many places to hide, and too little light to investigate clearly.

It would be impossible to climb through the ceiling. Shane would need to find the stairs and the proper way out. He got to his feet and looked around. He couldn't see a door in the darkness, but there had to be one.

As he finished a full-circle scan of the room, the ghost began to laugh.

CHAPTER 11

DEAD ON THE SHORE

Shane pushed bags of trash out of his way and headed to the closest wall. There were shelves mounted to the brick, and he paid them little mind at first as he followed them, looking for the break where he would find the door. It was only after passing two sets of shelves that he started to take notice of what he thought was clutter lining them.

Much of what was on the shelves looked like garbage, and that was not a surprise since someone had used the basement as a dump. There was an intention to the garbage on the shelves, though. Someone had placed each piece specifically.

Very few of the items seemed to relate to each other, and none of them belonged in a pharmacy. Shane saw a pocketknife, a gold ring, a small leather notebook, and an antique camera. All the items were damaged in some way, some so badly that they were little more than a jumble of pieces, like the camera.

The collection of trash made no sense to Shane until he scanned one of the lower shelves and saw an old blanket arranged haphazardly around some human remains. There was a skull and other bones, but they looked as though someone had smashed them with a sledgehammer.

Shane had seen the type of damage that the remains had sustained. He had destroyed enough ghosts that were bound to their remains to know what happened to them. The items on the shelf had been haunted items. The ghosts attached to them had been destroyed, and that destruction carried over to the items. These were the trophies that Beatrix collected, remnants of the ghosts she hunted. Or maybe they were just trophies for

Lanthimos, but the idea was the same.

Hinges creaked elsewhere in the basement, and Shane watched as a door slowly opened on the far side of the room. The dark wood moved very carefully as though the gentlest hand were pushing it open.

He could not see the ghost but knew it was there. The spirit was baiting him now, luring him closer. He saw no reason to let it down.

Shane left the shelf of haunted items behind and pushed the trash aside as he crossed the room to the door. By the time he got there, the door was fully open, leading into a smaller room and the staircase that led to another door.

The small room was empty except for a water heater against one wall and a series of filing cabinets on the other. Shane entered cautiously, looking for signs of the ghost. A hand grabbed him from behind, tangling in his collar as it pulled him back into the trash-filled room.

He hit the floor hard, and the rotting ghost was on top of him swiftly. With only one good hand, it had limited its attack options by grabbing hold of him. Shane grabbed its skeletal arm just above the elbow and pulled hard, dragging the ghost down until they were face to face.

Shane caught the ghost's head in his free hand, clutching it under the jaw. The spirit muttered in whatever language it spoke until Shane pushed up on its chin. It struggled and tried to use its handless arm for leverage but was unable to do so.

Kicking off with his feet, Shane rolled them over until he was on top. He let go of the ghost's arm and focused on the head. He pushed against the jaw with both hands, forcing the ghost's head back until its neck snapped. The spirit howled, a strangled and inhuman sound, and Shane kept pushing.

There was a pop as the head came free, then the entire thing burst. The force thrust Shane back toward the open door as one of the nearby shelves shuddered and collapsed when the item bound to the spirit came apart.

He rose to his feet slowly, taking a moment to catch his breath. In the room the ghost had opened, the filing cabinets against one of the walls drew his attention.

Many of them were empty, but Shane searched the drawers for relevant information. Much of what was left related to the pharmacy business. He found a file related to Lanthimos and the apartment he rented, but it was just an invoice for getting it painted from years ago.

As Shane rifled through documents, scanning for anything that stuck out, he flipped past a paper with a name that jumped out at him. Backtracking, he found a document that listed several names at the top. One of the names was Brandy Jean Talbot.

It was an invoice for the sale of the property. Brandy Jean Talbot and Lucas Hayes had been owners of the building, and a third party had sold it on their behalf, a law firm based out of Rhode Island. Brandy Jean Talbot's address was included in the filing.

"Tiverton, Rhode Island," Shane read aloud.

He took the paperwork with him and headed up the stairs. He was forced to break out of the pharmacy door onto the street. Fortunately, the neighborhood had not changed much since he had entered, and there was still no one around. He moved quickly away from the building, but not so fast as to make it look like he was fleeing a crime scene.

Tiverton was just across the state line. The drive took less than an hour, but finding the house was a more in-depth task. Shane couldn't find the street listed on the document even after crossing the town twice. Eventually, he was forced to pull over next to a roadside stand where an elderly man in overalls sold beets and farm-fresh eggs.

"I seem to be a bit lost; hoping you can help me," Shane said. "I'm looking for Strand Street."

The old man was reading a beaten-up copy of a Mack Bolan book and looked up at Shane from under the brim of his hat with a wide smile.

"Strand? Hell, no one goes that way these days. Can't find it 'cuz it don't exist no more," the man replied.

"The whole street?"

"The whole street," the old man confirmed. "I mean, it exists, but no one's there no more. Beach reclaimed most of it. Everyone had to pack up ages ago."

"Is there anything left?" Shane asked. "I had family who lived there when I was a kid. I've been overseas for a long time and lost touch."

"You serve?" the man asked.

Shane nodded and the man gestured to the north.

"That's where you want to go. Find Lenders Way and follow it down. There's no sign, but you'll see the road. Sandy, lots of trees. I gotta warn you, though, not many of them houses are still standing. Not sure what you're looking for, but you might just find beach."

"I appreciate that, sir," Shane said. "Just need to see it for myself, I guess."

"I hear ya," the man replied. "Have a care if the place is still standing. Nothing safe back there. The houses closest to the beach collapsed years ago. Dangerous if you head inside."

"I'll be careful. Thanks," Shane said.

Shane followed the old man's directions. Strand Street looked from the outside like a beach access as opposed to a road. It was already on the outskirts of town, right along the shore, and the drive took him farther from the town along a coastline of rocks, sand, and weeds.

The first sign of a house was about two hundred yards from where he entered. It was the frame of a building and a few planks still standing. The shore was nearly at the skeleton of what must have once been a large home. Shane could imagine in a storm that the water would have overtaken the property. There was not enough of it left to guess the address. He kept driving.

He passed two more broken-down frames of what had once been houses before finally coming to a property that was still standing. He continued down the sandy road, with the ocean on his left and weed-covered dunes on his right.

Shane rounded a curve and slowed his car as a slate-gray house on the beach came into view. The rear of the house was only a few yards from the waterline. Despite the closeness, the house appeared to be in good condition. Looks, of course, could be deceiving. He would have been surprised if the basement wasn't flooded all the time. The tide wasn't even in yet, and he assumed that the house would be partially submerged by nightfall.

As he passed the front of the house, he saw the address plastered to the siding next to the front door. He had found what he was looking for. Beatrix's house.

The driveway had vanished under sand, and random patches of long grass and some other weeds grew here and there. It looked like the house had risen from the beach, and there had never been a proper yard out front or back. It must have taken some time to get to that state, and Shane doubted anyone had lived there in over a decade.

Shane drove past the property and continued around the bend until he could no longer see the house before turning around and doubling back, parking near some trees that obscured him. From the road, he saw that some of the windows still had curtains hanging. Others were broken, and a few of the gray panels on the wall had been pulled free or maybe slipped loose in a storm. Half of the wraparound porch was covered in sand.

After his experience in Lanthimos' apartment, Shane was not willing to run in without getting the lay of the land. As it was, the sun would set in a couple of hours. He wanted to see if anyone came or went from the house, alive or otherwise. So, he waited until the sun set beyond the dunes.

The wind picked up, bringing the scent of salty air with it, and Shane watched the ocean as it grew darker until the light faded away, and he was in the black of night. He saw no movement from inside the house. Although he hadn't expected anyone to turn on a light, and the curtains didn't shift. There was no indication there was someone within, living or dead.

As the night wore on, the ocean began to encroach more on the beach. Waves came in, nothing fierce or destructive, but with enough force to reach the back side of the house.

Farther away, some distance from the house, movement at the edge of the water caught Shane's eye. He watched as a ghost dressed in a long coat emerged from the sea. It rose from the water and began walking along the shore, avoiding the house.

Shane couldn't make out the spirit clearly, but he could see it give the house a wide berth as it walked around the structure. The ghost was headed in Shane's general direction and would pass him on his right in a matter of minutes, though it gave no sign it either saw him or cared he was there.

With no other signs of life or death, Shane left the car and headed toward the ocean to intercept the spirit. It saw him coming but still paid no heed, not slowing its pace or altering course as it trudged along the waterline.

Up close, Shane saw the spirit was a man, drowned and pale with massive chunks of rubbery flesh missing across his face and hands. Much of his body was concealed beneath his saturated clothes. The water had distended his facial features, making it hard to judge how old he was when he'd drowned.

"Nice night for a stroll," Shane said when the ghost was close enough. The spirit stopped walking and blinked swollen eyes at him.

"Not really," the ghost answered. "Windy. Cloudy. Lonely. To each his own, huh?"

"Fair enough. You been here long?"

"Long enough that I don't know how long it's been," the ghost said. "Have we reached the millennium yet?"

Shane chuckled and nodded.

"You're a few decades late," he said.

The ghost cursed softly but shrugged.

"Doesn't matter, I suppose. Where are you headed?"

"I need to be in that house," Shane said. "You know anything about it?"

The ghost turned and looked back at the lonely structure, silent and dark on the shore.

"You don't want to be in that house. Unless you're looking to die."

CHAPTER 12

THE HOUSE OF SAND AND SORROW

The wind blew cool and crisp off the ocean. Shane saw distant lights to the northeast, across the bay in what must have been the very edge of Rhode Island or Massachusetts. It was a world away from this forgotten corner of sand and ruins.

"I'm looking for someone who lived there once. A woman named Beatrix, or maybe Brandy Jean," Shane told the spirit. The drowned man's expression didn't change, or if it did, the bloated flesh hid it well.

"I'm not here to make friends. Never was. Don't know anyone's name. Don't want to know yours," the ghost replied.

"Blonde woman. Maybe just a girl when she was here. Has a thing for shaving all or part of her head. She can see the dead. And she can hurt them," Shane said.

The ghost fell quiet, and even with the rot in his flesh, Shane saw he had become nervous. He shuffled his waterlogged feet and seemed to be consciously refusing to look toward the house.

"I know her. She lived here. Comes back now and then. When she does, I stay out there," the ghost said, pointing to the ocean. "Anyone with sense stays away."

"How often does she come here?"

"I don't know people's names, and I don't track their habits," the ghost said. "Sometimes she comes here, sometimes not. Months? Years? I don't pay any mind."

"What *can* you tell me?" Shane said. "I need to find this woman. And I need to stop her."

A gurgling sound came from deep in the ghost's lungs, and Shane realized it was a sigh.

"I don't interfere with her. I don't even let her know I'm here. She's dangerous. To me, to you, to anything that moves. And so is that damn house. I'm here because of that house. I'll be here forever because of that house, you understand me? Only reason I'm not trapped in those rotten walls with…"

He shook his head and Shane looked past him, to the shadowy building, and still saw nothing even as the waves lapped at the rear wall.

"The tide got my body. Pulled me into the ocean. Saved me from staying there forever. I avoid her, and I avoid *it*, and it's worked out well so far. See over there?"

The ghost turned to look out on the water and pointed to a series of low, jagged rocks around which the waves crashed.

"The rocks?" Shane asked.

The ghost nodded.

"I got pulled out there. My body was dragged by the undertow and deep currents in the tide. Wedged deep down in the dark. The fish came and nibbled away at every piece of me, bit by bit. Fish and eels and things that look like plants, and bugs that only come out at night when they can't be seen. They cleaned every inch of my bones, and my skull got wedged down there, right below the bottom of the tallest rock you see. Still there today. That's why she didn't get me. She can't find me down there. I'm safe. I'm this close, but I'm safe. But only because of that."

"You know what she'd do if she caught you?"

The ghost nodded again, still not looking at the house.

"Seen it before, once or twice, what she can do. She's mean. She's got a really cruel streak in her. Comes with the territory, I guess."

"What does that mean?" Shane asked.

"Means you don't want to go into the house. If there's one thing I know, it is that. You don't want to go into that house."

"What else is in the house?" Shane asked further.

The ghost shook his head.

"I've never gone inside. I never will. I've seen enough from out here. It's not just the girl, you know? She learned what she knows from the house. She's mean like she is because of the house."

"There's another ghost, then. Something from when she was young?"

"I told you I don't know. All I know is if you go inside that house, you are going to die. Everyone does."

"Beatrix didn't," Shane pointed out.

The ghost scoffed.

"Just barely. Listen to me or don't, I don't care. I'm not part of that place. I won't be."

The ghost tried to push past Shane, expecting to move through him, but bumped against his shoulder instead. He stopped in his tracks, his bloated, pale face looking as shocked as anyone Shane had ever seen.

"You're like them," the ghost whispered. He backed away, almost stumbled, and retreated into the ocean.

"Them? Them who?" Shane asked.

The ghost was already up to his waist in the water, his eyes locked on Shane as he shook his head.

"I'm not a part of it. You forget what I told you. Don't come looking for me. I'm not there. I'm not a part of any of this," he said, his voice almost frantic.

"I'm not coming for you," Shane said. "I'm just here—"

He didn't bother finishing. The waves washed over the ghost, and he was gone, down below back into the dark depths. It was never a good sign when a ghost was afraid of something. Not all were fighters, and some could panic as much as the living, but this sounded different. The house was not as empty as it looked.

Shane returned his attention to it, eyeing the building carefully from the shore. The waves crashed against the back of the house, over the wraparound porch, and against the walls. The house should have succumbed to the sea by now if it had stood as long as all the other broken-down husks of buildings Shane had seen on the shoreline. The ocean should have won the fight ages ago. But it hadn't.

The porch looked strong, and the walls looked solid. Time had come for the house; no one would think it was brand new, but it was falling apart in only the most superficial way. The siding and window shutters and stonework that crumbled were minor and aesthetic. The house persevered.

He approached in the dark, his feet sinking into the damp sand and slowing his progress. The sound of the waves was a constant soft roar, the background noise of the world.

He stayed just beyond the reach of the waves, where the sand was damp but not submerged. The house was unremarkable in every way. The look was ominous, but Shane could have said the same for a thousand homes that might or might not have been haunted.

The ocean ghost's implication was clear. Beatrix was not the danger. Or not the only one. But she was not even here. Something else was waiting behind the walls. But Shane's presence was not drawing it out, either.

He stared at the house, close enough that he could have put his hand on the railing of the wraparound porch. The windows of the upper floors were dark, and from the angle, he couldn't see anything inside. Nevertheless, the feeling that he was being observed had grown with each step. It was a needling, persistent sensation. Someone knew Shane was there.

If Beatrix had left something behind, then it was likely some kind of guard dog. Maybe that was exactly what it was; one of her twisted Hounds left in the building to protect it if someone came inside.

Shane did not want to tangle with something like that in the dark, unfamiliar place. It would be foolish to rush into a situation like that without an advantage.

He walked around the building, checking every window he saw. Nothing in the house gave itself away. But the feeling of eyes on him was so intense that, by the time he reached the front of the house, he felt like he could turn around and be face to face with whoever was watching him.

Shane reached out and touched the banister next to the sand-covered steps that led up to the front door. The wood felt dry, and white paint flaked off under his palm. The wood was smooth otherwise, and solid to the touch. It did not feel cold to the touch, and there was nothing ominous about it. The house didn't react to his presence. Nothing lunged from the shadows to defend itself.

He stared at the front door. Like many beach houses, there was a screen door over a heavier wooden door behind. The screen door was mostly white, flaking like the banisters, and there was dark wood beyond like the siding of the house. A window was set into the heavier wooden door. The glass looked black from his vantage point. There could have been someone standing there looking back at him, and he wouldn't have seen it.

The ocean ghost had given Shane no specifics about why he needed to avoid the house, but he was also adamant in his warning. The house was dangerous, and it would kill him. Shane had no reason to doubt the ghost's sincerity.

There were none of the typical signs of a haunting. No unexplained sounds and no shadowy movements. No gust of cold air tickled the back of his neck. The house did nothing to entice him to enter or to scare him off. Despite that, Shane felt with absolute certainty that it was waiting for him. The house, or whatever was in the house, was patient. It was calm and cool and felt no sense of urgency. Shane felt it in his gut.

He took a step back. Nothing happened. He took another step back. The calmness around the house remained. The gentle crash of the ocean was still the only sound he heard.

Shane had been to many haunted houses in his lifetime. He had experienced all the ways a ghost manifested and staked their claim to a place. There was something wrong with Beatrix's house. He could see nothing wrong, and he could hear nothing wrong. It was just a feeling, and it lacked any specificity. It aggravated him even more that he couldn't put his finger on what it was.

Something was different about the house. Different from other hauntings he had experienced. Even though he had yet to see a ghost on the premises or feel anything, he couldn't deny the sensation that had taken hold in his gut and twisted like a knife.

"What the hell happened here?" Shane asked aloud. The house offered no answer.

He turned and walked away from the building. The sense of being watched stuck with him, and it took some effort not to look back over his shoulder to make sure he wasn't being followed. He knew he wasn't, as sure as he knew something was still watching him from that place. It just wanted to make him think that, and he wouldn't give it the satisfaction of looking back as though he were afraid. He wouldn't acknowledge that whatever the house was doing had worked.

Shane headed back down the road toward his car. The feeling subsided as he walked beyond the line of sight of the house and slipped behind the trees he had used as cover for the vehicle. He didn't feel it watching because it couldn't watch anymore.

He would not go into the house at night. A ghost didn't need the darkness to kill anyone, but it was an advantage he didn't need to give whatever awaited him. He would head in when the sun rose and the light prevented whatever was inside from hiding further. If the house wanted to play games, it would at least play games on Shane's terms. If, as the ghost from the ocean had said, the house wanted to kill him, Shane would face it in the light.

CHAPTER 13

THE TIGHTENING OF THE NOOSE

Molly's Pub smelled of old beer and sweat. The air conditioning died three summers before, and no one had gotten around to fixing it. The regulars were content to swelter in the dark, dirty basement so long as they had a cold beer to temper it. Maybe "content" was the wrong word. They were willing to endure. Where else would they go?

Beatrix had been going to the pub for as long as she could remember. The pub was the kind of place that nobody would go to if they didn't have to. Decent people didn't go there to drink. It survived because it had a small but loyal customer base, but also mostly because the owner was involved in a number of illegal activities, and it was a reasonable place to launder money. Beatrix liked that.

She sat in a corner booth, facing the door, drinking a bottle of Canadian beer, and eating stale peanuts from an unsanitary bowl. The door opened, letting in the neon lights of the pink sign that hung over it in the alley.

The man who entered was bathed in a pink glow before the door closed and he was trapped in the dimly lit haze with everyone else. Beatrix simply stared at him.

Adrian Lanthimos had never been her friend. He thought he was. If he wasn't a useful set of hands that Beatrix could rely on to carry things, drive vehicles, and make sure everything was where it needed to be, she probably would have killed him.

Times had changed, of course. Adrian no longer fancied himself the knight in shining armor that would save Beatrix from the monsters that lurked in the shadows. He had learned, hard though the lessons might have been, that she wasn't going to love him. She could see he still hoped for something. Maybe she would soften to him. Maybe she would let him in and share her deepest, darkest secrets, and they'd fall madly in love. It was hard to decide if she wanted to laugh or vomit.

He came to the booth where she sat and slid in across from her with his back to the door.

"We have a problem," he said, his voice low.

Adrian never raised his voice. He was a picture of calm. She knew it was all fake. He wanted to project strength. He wanted to be the cool and mysterious ghost hunter. It was laughable.

"When don't we?" she said, taking a drink from her beer.

"It's Ryan. He found the pharmacy. I've got him on camera breaking in."

Beatrix took another drink. Shane Ryan finding Adrian's old haunt was about as surprising as beer being wet.

"Is that it?"

"You don't think that's important?" he asked.

"I don't know. Did he not take off his shoes before walking on the carpet? What do I care if he found a condemned pharmacy?"

"Birch was there. What if Ryan destroyed him?"

Beatrix rolled her eyes. Once upon a time, Kelly Birch was a Harvester, until he got a bit too big for his britches. Ten thousand dollars and some stab wounds later, he was dead on a mattress with his ghost haunting Adrian's old apartment.

"Good," she said.

"Good?"

Adrian spat the word. He was losing his cool veneer. She loved it when that happened. He could never play his cool guy role for long when she baited him.

"Birch was an asshole, Adrian. In case you forgot."

"We had a line on him for a hunt, Bea. He could have easily pulled in a hundred thousand. Or is this not about the business anymore? Did you stop caring about that, too?"

Beatrix finished her beer and set the empty bottle loudly on the table. The bartender, a beast of a man named Hank, looked over and nodded, passing a fresh bottle to the waitress.

"Two things, Adrian. One, don't call me Bea or I will cut your face. Two, stop whining about how I feel. You sound like a therapist, and if I wanted a therapist, I'd go kill one and beat a conversation out of his ghost."

Adrian sighed dramatically, shaking his head as he leaned back on the seat. The waitress brought Beatrix a new beer and left without asking Adrian if he wanted anything.

"If you don't care about Birch, how about the Scarecrow? How about Swamp Guts? And Leech? Ryan destroyed all three of them."

"He found Leech out in the woods? That's wild," she replied, starting in on the new beer.

"You're unbelievable," Adrian said softly. "That's half a million, at least. Half a goddamn million! What the hell are we even doing anymore?"

"We have more," she said. The thing about ghosts was that there were always more. And if there weren't, you could kill people until you got one. They were an exceptionally renewable resource.

"Seriously?" Adrian said. She could feel the disgust emanating from him, and she couldn't hold in her laughter.

"Lighten up, Adrian. You're going to give yourself an ulcer or high blood pressure or something. You're not impressed by any of this? He's good, don't you think? Leech was gross; I didn't even want to touch that guy. I had to deal with him when I was a kid in that house. I'm glad he's gone. And Swamp Guts, too? I might ask Ryan for his autograph before I kill him."

"And if he kills you first?" Adrian countered.

Beatrix took a long drink, draining the whole bottle. She slammed it down again.

"If he kills me, then I'll be dead, and I won't have to listen to your tough-guy act anymore. I don't see how I can lose."

His hands balled into fists, and her smile broadened. Adrian was easy to bait but not always easy to anger. She liked knowing she could push him so far.

His face was flush, and his eyes stared with intensity. He was as angry as she had seen him. The laughter that came from her only made it worse, and that made her laugh even more.

"Everything might be a joke to you, Bea, but it's not to me. This was supposed to be about the money. If you want to be a reckless basket case, you can do it on your time with your money."

The smile never left her face. Her hand jerked, knocking the bottle down hard enough on the table to break it. Adrian barely had time to react before she was on her feet, leaning across the table with the shard of brown glass in her hand. She dragged the edge across Adrian's face from his cheekbone to his lip, splitting the flesh so deeply that blood flowed out in a sheet.

"Jesus," he gasped, reeling back, and covering the wound as she returned to her seat.

"Don't forget your place, Adrian. You ride in the bitch seat; I'm the one driving. And I told you not to call me Bea."

Blood ran over his fingers. No one in the bar reacted to her outburst, even though the scattered few patrons and the bartender had seen it. No one questioned Beatrix there. They had seen her lose her temper.

"There will be nothing left to drive if Shane Ryan keeps pulling everything apart," he told her, standing his ground. "He's not a joke. You can't treat him like one."

"Jesus Christ on a bike, Adrian," Beatrix said dramatically. "Of course, he is. Everything is a joke. The fact you don't see it is the biggest joke of all."

They stared at each other in silence while Beatrix waited for Adrian to say something else. He wasn't always as stupid as he looked, and this time, he simply stared back, meeting her gaze without a word.

Beatrix took some money from her pocket and set it on the table. She got up from her seat and walked to Adrian's side.

"Stop worrying so much, Adrian. You'll live longer," she said.

The last thing she needed was Adrian telling her what she needed to do or when she needed to do it. Of course, Solo had gone off half-cocked and tracked down a few of their ghosts. So what? At least he was keeping busy. He could run up and down the East Coast for all she cared; none of it would change her plans. Adrian should have known that by now.

She left the bar, walking out into the pink neon entryway in the otherwise dark, damp alley before heading to her left. She had no destination in mind, she was just going where the night took her.

Adrian got up from his seat and wandered across the bar to the restroom. The bartender glanced at him but said nothing, nor did anyone else. They had all seen him there before, and they knew who he worked with. They tolerated him as much as he tolerated them.

The bathroom was as dingy as the rest of the bar. It smelled like a mixture of urine and urinal cakes, each odor battling to overcome the other. The walls were marred with graffiti, obscenities scrawled with Sharpie markers, and numerous stains from who knew what over the years.

He stepped to the mirror over the single sink and looked at his face on the foggy surface. He pulled his hand away and could see the blood still running from the gash in his cheek, down his neck, and soaking his shirt. He turned on the faucet, rinsed his hand, and then washed his face. The blood still flowed freely, and he realized he needed stitches.

The paper towel machine rattled noisily as he pumped the lever until a suitable amount of paper came out, which he tore off and folded up. He used it as an impromptu bandage to apply pressure to the wound with one hand as he pulled his phone free of his pocket with the other.

Adrian had known Beatrix for a long time. They had endured a lot together and, for Adrian, that bred loyalty. They were partners. They were supposed to be, anyway. But as time went on, Beatrix proved herself to be more unhinged, more detached from the real world and him. There was a time when he would have given his life for her. He didn't think he felt that way anymore.

The Harvesters started with a clear goal in mind: Make money and destroy ghosts. It was a simple concept and a lucrative one. No one needed the dead walking around. But they both needed money. Once they realized how they could combine the two, it was like winning the lottery.

Beatrix had always had secrets. The people she talked to. Places she went. She had lied about a lot of things, from way back at the beginning. It had never affected their work, and Adrian had never cared about it. Everyone had secrets. But things had changed.

He put the phone to his ear and waited as he listened to the other end ring. The ringing stopped as the phone clicked. Silence answered him.

"I need the Houndmaster," he said.

CHAPTER 14

INTO THE BREACH

The sun rose over the ocean and light slashed across the land as though cleaning it of the night's mysteries. Nothing had disturbed the house. No one came, and no one left. The ghost from the sea did not return. If Shane waited any longer, he would just be spinning his wheels.

He left the car and made the short walk to the sand-covered property. He saw some sailboats in the distance, barely rising above the horizon. People out on the water to enjoy the sunrise and experience the day as it arrived with no distractions.

Closer to where he was, there were still no signs of life. No one from town seemed to travel that way early or late even though the beaches looked very inviting. The houses—or what were left of them—must have put people off. There was something about ghost towns, or in this case, a ghost street, that made people uncomfortable even if there was no reason for it.

Shane approached the house, trudging through the loose sand, and climbed the steps to the front door. The screen was rusted and malformed, and the lightweight door came off the hinges in his hands. He leaned it against the wall and tried the sturdier wooden door behind it.

The door opened easily, unlocked and not even stiff. Shane pushed it in and stepped into the house. The interior was sandy, and though not nearly as bad as the outside, there was still a layer covering the carpet. He entered a hallway that led straight toward the living room, brightly lit with floor-to-ceiling windows that looked onto the ocean at the back of the house. The curtains on either side were held back with little ties, allowing as much light into the room as possible.

The rising sun was framed perfectly. An artist couldn't have painted a better picture of the scene. It must have been a hell of a view every morning when people lived there.

An odor in the house reminded Shane of a spice shop or scented candles. It was better than what he had encountered at Lanthimos' apartment, but he couldn't source it to anything specific.

Shane walked down the hallway, passing several closed doors to get to the living room and get the full view of the window and the sunrise beyond. The ocean was right up to the back door, just barely above the surface of the wraparound porch that the sliding glass door would have let out onto. He saw a stain along the bottom of the glass from where waves had crashed against it and left a residue of salt and vegetation.

The house was still fully furnished, but it was clear no one had lived there for a long time. Layers of sand and dust covered the chairs, coffee table, and sofa. The corners of the room away from direct sunlight were entombed in cobwebs that hung in streamers from the old ceiling fan and the tops of several hutches in the room.

In the far corners, against the wall into which the window was set, the cobwebs were clogged with dust and debris. The result was a cluster of beige, gossamer fluff that stretched from the ceiling halfway down the wall.

The floorboards creaked underfoot as Shane walked around the room. He opened the doors of one of the old hutches and looked inside at an arrangement of knickknacks and things like decorative plates and pewter figurines. Everything was dusty, and nothing had been touched in a long time.

There was a room off the living room, and Shane headed inside. It had been a dining room once upon a time, and the table was still there with eight chairs set up. The walls were decorated with a vaguely nautical theme, including an old wooden wheel from a ship, and some large, knotted rope. A vase on the table was filled with flowers that had long ago rotted away to black stems and withered leaves that were ensconced in cobwebs.

Shane went from the dining room toward the kitchen, which turned him back toward the front of the house. The kitchen was open, but shutters covered the windows, and it was darker than the first two rooms he inspected.

He opened the door of the large, teal General Electric refrigerator that looked like it must have come from the seventies. There was no power, and the inside of the fridge smelled like mold. There were some old bottles on the shelves, things with stained labels that he couldn't read. Something black had spilled on the bottom but had long ago dried out. He closed the door and left the kitchen, heading down a hallway toward a closed door.

Shane investigated the house from room to room and found nothing interesting. If there were ghosts in the house, they stayed out of his way. Nothing moved, not even the cobwebs.

He made his way to a flight of stairs, its dark wood the first surface he had seen inside without a layer of sand. The staircase rose and then curved left to vanish onto the second floor. He saw nothing from below except for the edge of a hallway with more closed doors.

The first step squealed when he stepped on it, the wood sliding down the length of one of the nails that held it in place. Each subsequent step produced a new sound, a grown or a creak, as Shane's weight distressed the panel.

He took the stairs slowly, watching the railing along the second floor as he made his way up. There were more cobwebs up there, and more dust, but nothing moved. No ghosts, not even a cool breeze.

He reached the top of the steps and stood in the hallway. It branched left and right, with the ugly, multicolor carpet dulled and muted by the dust that covered it. The window facing east at the end of the hall was shuttered, but light still came in around it. To the west, the window looking out over the front of the house was concealed behind thin curtains.

Shane started at the west end and approached the first door. He turned the knob and entered a musty room with shuttered windows and little light. The place smelled of cigarette smoke and age. A bed was pressed to the wall farthest from the door, and there was an ashtray that had been filled with cigarette butts to the point of absurdity. Many more had fallen on the floor around it. There had to be hundreds.

The mattress was stained yellow from years of sweat and maybe more. Old socks and shirts and some torn jeans were scattered about. Crushed beer cans were piled not far from the cigarettes, along with some weathered magazines like People and US Weekly that dated back to the nineties.

He checked the closet and found a few more clothing items and some water-damaged books. No paperwork, no photographs, and nothing about who once lived there or where they'd gone.

Shane continued down the hall, checking room after room. Many were full of cigarette butts and old beer cans. Some were decorated more in line with an older person. The choice of decor and bedding was the only change from room to room. Everything looked like it had been abandoned and then squatters had moved in for some time afterward.

He stood in the doorway of another bedroom, this one with blue walls and nautical theme. There was more garbage there, but the smell was dry and old. There were more magazines in the room as well, and Shane had a thought.

It was not a very in-depth thought, nothing of importance, but it made him stop. How many rooms had he gone through since he had seen those magazines? At least six.

Shane turned around and looked back at the hallway. The stairs were only a few paces behind him. The window that overlooked the front of the house was just two rooms back. How had he been through at least six bedrooms already?

The pages of one of the magazines rustled as a faint breeze stirred in the room. Cigarette butts rolled, and suddenly the door slammed behind him. Shane turned quickly, grabbing the knob, and opening it again. There was no resistance, no attempt to keep him in the room. But when the door opened, the hallway was different.

No stairs waited for Shane on the other side. The windows at either end of the hall were gone. In fact, there was no end to the hall. The passage stretched on to his left and right.

There was light in the hallway, but it didn't come from any source he could identify. With no windows and no light fixtures, the whole place should have been dark, but it wasn't. All he could see was the dusty carpet and door after door after door in both directions.

Shane grunted, nodding as he took a moment to appreciate the situation. He reached into his pocket and pulled out his pack of cigarettes, taking one and placing it between his lips before lighting it. Beatrix's home was more like the house on Berkley Street than he had realized.

With the stairs missing, Shane suspected that no matter which room he went into, he would only end up where the house wanted him to be. If there was a window, it would not open. It would probably not even break. He was trapped in the house for now.

Shane's house was motivated by two things. The first was aggression. The house fought threats and did so violently. The second was self-preservation. If the house could not overcome a threat, it would get rid of it. He hoped that Beatrix's house worked the same way.

Trailing cigarette smoke behind him, Shane turned what should have been east and walked down the hall. He let the doors pass unopened, not interested in what lay behind them. To the left and right, the identical doors remained closed, and he ignored them.

He had traveled far enough that he should have been a hundred yards into the ocean already, but the hallway still stretched ever forward with no end in sight. Shane didn't rush or panic; he didn't do anything except walk and smoke.

He had been impressed by the patience of whatever waited in the house the previous night. It didn't give itself away. Whatever spirit lived there, it had not made a move since Shane had entered except for sealing him into the never-ending hall. He couldn't overlook the possibility that the house would let him wander forever. The same fate had befallen Eloise at the Anderson House. Once she was trapped in the walls, it kept her there until thirst and starvation overcame her. The dead could be extremely patient. So, too, could a house of the dead.

The feeling he got in Beatrix's house was different from the feeling in his home. At first, he attributed that to the fact that his home was not out to get him, but he wasn't sure that was true. If houses had personalities, Beatrix's house had a different one than his. Still, it was just a feeling, and it was hard to explain.

In some ways, he felt like it was not dissimilar from his ability to identify a ghost just by looking at it. While many spirits bore the wounds of their demise and some looked like little more than rotting corpses, others like Carl did not give themselves away so easily. But there was still some indefinable quality, that Shane could identify with just a glance.

He was never wrong when it came to picking a ghost out of a crowd. That same feeling was overwhelmingly what he felt in the house. He understood something about it. It did not have the patience of the house on Berkley Street. It would not play for long if it didn't think Shane was falling for its tricks. His indifference to being trapped would have an effect because the house wanted him to react.

Shane finished his cigarette and started a second. When that one was done, he started a third. And then a fourth. His biggest fear now was that he would run out of cigarettes before he ran out of hallway. The pack has been nearly fresh, though. He still had fourteen sticks to go.

He had walked for hours when finally, the house had enough. Ahead of him, one of the doors slowly swung open out into the hallway. The foundation of the house rumbled, a soft shake as though settling, but it was the first real reaction he got from the house since he'd been there.

It was done playing games.

CHAPTER 15

ESCAPE ROOM

Shane stood in the hallway and looked into the open room. It was not a bedroom and it was not a small, messy space full of cigarette butts and old magazines like the other rooms had been. Instead, he found himself looking at the living room. The sun had risen high enough that it was no longer framed by the big, sliding glass doors that made up the eastern wall, but otherwise, everything was the same.

The cobwebs in the corner shifted in the faintest of breezes. That was different. There had been no airflow at all before. And though it was extremely limited now, creating barely imperceptible movement, it was still something new.

Shane stepped across the threshold and into the living room. The cobwebs swayed again, the result of a single shift in the air current. He turned and looked behind him, and the front door was gone. There was no other way out of the room even though it had had two entrances the first time he visited. The sliding glass door was still there, though.

He approached it and looked out. Shane could no longer see the wraparound porch, just the ocean. There was no sign of land to the north as there had been before, and no shoreline across the bay.

"That's a good trick," he said out loud. His house couldn't do that.

Maybe if the pond in the yard were bigger.

Shane grabbed the handle and tried to slide the door open, but it wouldn't budge. He put his other hand against the frame and leaned into it, pushing as hard as he could. There wasn't even an inch of wiggle.

Changing tactics, Shane took a step back and then kicked, slamming his heel against the pane of glass. His foot hit hard, and the glass vibrated. He kicked again and again, but the glass held fast.

He left the door and crossed the room to the hutch he had investigated earlier. Inside were several brass figurines and ornaments. The largest and heaviest was a brass seal on the side of a small candlestick holder. The seal's flippers held the candle snuffer, and the whole thing weighed several pounds. Shane took it off the shelf and hurled it across the room at the glass door.

The ornament hit with a *thunk* and then fell harmlessly to the floor. Shane walked to it, picked it up, and slammed it against the glass. He pounded against the window with it, but he might as well have been trying to break through a brick wall. The house was not ready to let him leave. He would have to change its mind.

Shane returned to the wall where the entrance to the room should have been. He picked up the coffee table from the center of the room and slammed it down on the floor, shattering the wood. He broke the remaining pieces apart until he had a table leg free and then used that to beat the wall.

The house rumbled again, shifting beneath his feet and expressing dissatisfaction as he destroyed the drywall and tore a hole through where the doorway had once been. The structure crumbled easily, and Shane began kicking the lower portions, making the hole bigger as he pushed through to the other side.

Darkness waited beyond the wall, not that he expected to find the exit so easily. If the house was interested in playing games, he would make it work hard to keep up with him.

He stepped through the opening and found himself in a room with a peaked ceiling, what must have been the attic. Light came through a tiny octagonal window on one wall but was mostly obscured by slats of wood laid horizontally across it.

A skeleton was propped against the wall under the window. It was partially covered in rags, the decayed remains of clothing that had long ago been devoured by the elements. Now they were just dry, dusty fragments hanging from the bones.

The skull faced Shane. Patches of dried flesh were still stuck to it, shriveled by time and temperature. Wisps of gray hair were still attached to the scalp, kinked and standing at odd angles.

At first glance, it might have passed for a dead body, but Shane could see that it was not someone's physical remains. It was a spirit, desiccated though it might have been.

Shane did nothing. He watched the ghost and waited for it to make the first move. It took longer than he expected and did not come as he had expected it to, either. Rather than moving, or even speaking, the ghost heaved a long, tired sigh.

The sound had a hollow quality, coming from deep in a chest that had no capacity to hold air. Nevertheless, it sounded breathy and exhausted.

"You... should... not... have... come... here..."

The ghost had to force out each word, and it sounded like the effort was immense. Its voice was soft and sounded far away.

"So I've been told," Shane replied.

"This... is a place... for death. You... can't be alive... and leave."

"Beatrix left. She's still alive. Or maybe you know her as Brandy Jean," Shane replied.

The empty eyes fixed on Shane, and the spirit sighed again.

"This... is... a... tomb. You... will join... us."

Shane looked around and saw no one else. The other spirits of the house, if there were any, were still playing their cards close to the chest. Maybe they wanted to get more of an idea of who Shane was and what he could do before they showed themselves.

"I'm just here to find Beatrix," Shane said. "We have unfinished business."

"She was... made. Forged," the ghost said. "If she... comes back...

there will be… no remorse. No pity."

"Forged? What does that mean?" Shane asked.

"She is… Mr. Shadow's right hand. And you… are nothing."

"Who is Mr. Shadow?"

"She is… his righteous wrath. You are… only… meat."

"Who is Mr. Shadow? Is that who's been giving her information?" Shane asked.

"She is… the scythe. You are… wheat… to be… reaped."

"I get it. Lots of fun metaphors," Shane said, stepping closer to the skeletal figure. "Tell me about Mr. Shadow."

The ghost produced another long, drawn-out sigh. The empty eyes still seemed fixed on Shane, though the head had not moved.

"It would be… better… to die now," the ghost said. "I can… save you… much pain."

The ghost braced itself against the wall. Slowly, awkwardly, it began to rise, dragging itself into an upright position. Shane watched and waited, unsure if the ghost was playing possum or if it really was that slow. It gave no sign of a trick. It moved like it looked, decrepit and decayed.

"Such pain… is not… for you," the ghost said.

It took a shaky step forward, and Shane waited. Only two paces separated them. The ghost raised its skinless arms, unsteady and shaking as it reached for him.

"This won't work," he told the ghost. "Just tell me about this Mr. Shadow, and you can go right back to your nap."

"Your blood… will flow…"

Another step forward, and it was within reach. The skeletal hands grasped clumsily. Shane batted the ghost aside and pushed it against the wall, back the way it had come.

The ghost kept coming. There was no urgency or effort behind anything it did. Like the breathy sighs that it heaved, it seemed like it was just too tired or indifferent to care.

"Do not... fight... inevitability..."

"I think you and I have different definitions of that word," Shane said.

He waited for the ghost to come at him again. The second attack was identical to the first. It didn't even do something else, come at him from another angle, or trick him in any way.

This time, Shane caught the ghost by the wrists and refused to let it advance. It struggled in his grip in the most rudimentary way. There was no strength behind its movements and no effort to break free. It was like holding back a small child.

"Succumb... to... your fate," it sighed.

"Tell me about Mr. Shadow," Shane insisted. The ghost acted as though it couldn't hear him speaking, pushing meekly to get a grip on him again.

Frustrated, Shane pulled the ghost's right arm from its socket. It came away with little effort and faded to nothing in his hand in a blink.

The ghost had no reaction. But the house did not let it go unnoticed. The floor shook beneath his feet like a low-grade earthquake. Dust fell in streams from the ceiling as though sand was filtering through unseen holes in the roof. The foundation groaned, and the limited light coming through the cracks in the attic began to dim.

"He calls... for you," the skeleton moaned. "You... will feed... the engine... of chaos."

"You have to be kidding me." Shane rolled his eyes.

He had met his share of dramatic spirits, but this one seemed too committed to the bit. Keeping it restrained was not difficult, but he didn't have time to babysit a spirit that was not willing to answer his questions and wanted to—very weakly—try to destroy him.

"Last chance, buddy. Tell me where to find Mr. Shadow. Is he in the house?"

"You don't... find him... he finds... you. And he... already has," the ghost said.

Shane pushed the ghost back again, giving it one final opportunity to stand down. It did not take it.

The spirit stumbled forward, reaching with his remaining hand. The skull's mouth fell open and out came a dry, throaty growl. Shane took the ghost by the wrist and pulled back, forcing the ghost forward.

The skull crunched and snapped under the force of the blow. It fell loose from the ghost's body and flipped end over end as it tumbled back. The body burst, buffeting Shane with a blast of energy that was far weaker than what he usually experienced.

He had not expected to destroy the ghost with such a simple attack and was surprised that it came apart so easily. The house surged beneath his feet, shifting as though the building was coming down. Shane was knocked forward as the house began to list, the floor lifting at a forty-five-degree angle.

Shane collided with the front wall and the small, octagonal window. The wooden slats covering it had fused, transforming it from a window to a panel on the wall. The light was snuffed out all around him, and he found himself in darkness as the old, forgotten items of the attic tumbled forward with the movement of the house.

Shane struggled to grab hold of something to steady himself and maintain his balance in the darkness. The house continued to move, the angle shifting and the floor under his feet giving way as he tumbled in another direction.

Things hit him in the dark. Boxes, furniture, and unseen objects large and small crashed into him as they tumbled together. It felt like the house was rolling down a hill with Shane inside. All he could do was reach out for anything to hold onto, but there was nothing there.

Shane was tossed forward and fell on his face onto a dusty, dry floor. The movement stopped, the house was no longer rolling, and Shane got to his hands and knees. He braced himself for another round, but the house had finished whatever it was doing.

"Shane."

The voice was a distant whisper, not one that he recognized.

"Shane Ryan."

This was another voice, closer than the first one, deeper and more insistent.

"Shane."

"Shane."

"Shane Ryan."

"Shane."

"Shane Ryan!"

New voices joined. First just a couple, then a dozen, then more than Shane could count. Some were so close that he could feel their breath against his ear, cold and dead. Others seemed so far away that it was hard to tell if he was imagining them. They filled the darkness all around him.

They said nothing but his name over and over again. Some sounded desperate for help. Others were lurid and enticed him to come forward. Some were hateful, some were angry. More joined until the dark space was a chorus, a symphony of dead voices crying out for one thing.

Shane Ryan.

CHAPTER 16
BURNED AND BROKEN

Shane got to his feet, ignoring the hundreds of voices calling for him. If there were any ghosts in the darkness, he could not see them or feel them moving around him. Even when the voices came close, there was nothing there when he reached out.

It was too dark to see even a hand in front of his face. He could feel the floor beneath his feet but could not find a wall even after walking with his arms extended.

Everything that had previously been in the attic was gone. Shane was in an open, empty space. Without light, he had no idea which direction to walk, assuming there was a right direction to go.

The voices were becoming more urgent and more frantic. They yelled his name, hissed it, and shouted it near and far. The situation would escalate soon enough, and something would confront him in the darkness. He didn't want to fight whatever he was dealing with on its terms.

Shane slammed his foot down. The floorboards shuddered and creaked. He slammed his heel down again, and something cracked. The voices were silenced immediately.

In the newfound quiet, Shane could hear his heartbeat pounding in his ears. He hammered the floorboard with his foot again and again until the wood broke. Instead of a single board breaking to give him access to whatever was below, the floor buckled beneath him. The floorboards gave in, and Shane fell.

He landed on his back in about two feet deep water that was cold as ice. The temperature drop was a shock and he gasped, nearly drawing in a mouthful as he lifted his head to get away from the chill.

Shane sat briefly, orienting himself. The light had returned above him at the edges of a spacious room. It filtered in through cracks, illuminating the area enough to let him see he was in the basement.

The floor was uneven, and the water deepened toward the wall directly ahead of him. He moved back and the level decreased until he was barely submerged a foot. Cigarette butts and empty cans floated on the surface, more trash like he'd seen elsewhere in the house, along with bits of wood and plastic.

Shane got to his feet, dripping and half frozen, and trudged across the basement until he was standing on dry cement. The span of dry land was limited, a strip about six feet wide against the farthest wall.

The trash on the dry patch of floor was densely concentrated. One corner held a massive pile of cigarette butts, as though someone had sat there for years smoking endlessly and tossing them aside. There were thousands, all the same brand, stacked several feet tall in the center of the wide mound.

A thin wisp of smoke still rose from the pile. Shane could see no sign of the smoker. If someone had been there, they were hidden. The smell remained, oddly intense for a single butt left burning, and the rich, deep smell of tobacco cut through the undertone of seawater.

There were no obvious doors, stairs, or windows through which to escape. The walls and floors were concrete, and kicking his way out as he had done in the attic would not help. He did not want to venture into the water again if he didn't have to. Aside from the temperature, anything could have been hiding in there, waiting to drag him under. No need to give the ghosts another advantage unless he had to.

He walked the length of the dry cement floor, looking for something to help him escape, or even for what reason the house had dropped him there. By the time he made his way back to the mound of cigarette butts, the wisp of smoke rising from it had grown thicker.

A pair of cigarette butts tumbled down the side of the pile and rolled across the floor into the water. Shane watched as more slipped from the pile and hit the ground. Something moved in the center of the mass, disturbing the butts and feeding the smoke that rose and filled the space.

As the butts fell away, Shane saw a pile of ash exposed underneath. Yellow filters and white paper were cast aside, leaving only the salt-and-pepper gray of the ashes and the smoke that rose in tendrils.

The ashes jostled next, and Shane expected to see something rise from them. Instead, the ashes themselves moved, rising slowly as though being lifted by an unseen force. The remainder of the butts sloughed away, and the ashes took the form of something close to human. Arms, legs, and a head were all roughly formed and lacking detail, like a figure hastily cast from clay or wax.

Gaps in the malformed head opened into a wide chasm of a mouth that filled with rolling smoke, and then two smaller holes. Orange embers burned in each, a rudimentary representation of eyes. The ash monster belched smoke in a low, angry roar, and the eyes flared brightly.

"All you need to do is tell me about Mr. Shadow," Shane said.

Smoke poured from the spirit's ashen mouth like gray vomit, light as air, and flowed away in small tendrils. It reached Shane, and he batted it away with his hand, feeling a distinct, sharp burn where it touched his flesh.

He winced and nodded, understanding the stakes.

"Come for me, then," he told the manifestation.

The ghost obliged, lumbering forward on thick legs of ash. It shed gray dust with each step, the fine particles drifting away and settling all around as it stormed toward him. Shane ducked before it reached him, cupping his hands in the cold water that filled the basement and throwing a handful into the ash creature's face.

The water splashed into the ashes with a hiss that made the burning eyes fizzle. The shape started to collapse as though melting, the water blending with the ash and creating a dark, muddy slop. The spirit roared, spewing smoke, and Shane rushed at it, sweeping its legs from beneath it so that it fell.

More ashes burst free in a cloud of dust. Shane was at its side immediately. He pushed a boot into the amorphous, gray body and thrust it toward the water. The spirit skidded and flailed, panicking as it realized what Shane was doing. Its attempts to save itself were too little too late.

The cold water of the basement lapped at the ash creature's side, stripping away the substance that made it what it was. It tried to crawl free, to twist away, and Shane kicked it again, knocking it fully into the water.

Muddy ashes splashed and splattered about. The thing fought as though it had been dipped in acid, struggling to escape its fate. The ashes were pulled from it within seconds, stripping the fake body it had created and revealing the ghost within.

What remained was smaller and more delicate, but no less inhuman. The ghost had burned to death, and it had been severe. Black, crisped flesh coated the spirit. Many of the wounds on its body were fractures, breaks in the flesh that cracked and oozed, revealing blood and pus within. It was caked in serum from burst blisters that had dried around the wound edges.

Smoke rose from the ghost's wounds as it pulled itself out of the water and got to its feet. It stared at Shane with engorged, milk-white eyes. They had been cooked as much as the body had been, almost to the point of bursting. The ghost was unable to close them, assuming it still had eyelids left to try.

As it stood, Shane saw that the severe burns were limited to the upper half of the body, from the chest up. Below that, the burns were not as severe, but they were intentional. There were a series of circular burns across the ghost's abdomen and down its thighs.

Shane had seen cigarette burns in flesh and recognized them for what they were. While some could have been self-inflicted, more circled the ghost's abdomen and across its back, which he saw as it gained its footing. Someone had tortured whoever the ghost had been when they were alive, and then, from the looks of things, had killed them by setting their head on fire.

Aside from the burns, the ghost was incredibly thin. Shane could see its ribs where the burns had not destroyed flesh. Its thighs were barely as big around as Shane's biceps, indicating the person it once was had been malnourished to the point of starvation, likely over a long period.

"I'm looking for Brandy Jean. Or Mr. Shadow. Is that who did this to you?" Shane asked.

The ghost screamed. There were no words, only a high-pitched, bloodcurdling shriek like something he'd expect to hear from a person being murdered. It rushed at Shane faster than he had anticipated and with great strength behind it.

The ghost dropped its shoulder and collided with Shane. Thin, charred arms wrapped around his body and clawed at his back while Shane slammed an elbow into the spirit's neck at the base of its skull.

They fell entangled to the floor together, each fighting to remain on top of the other and hold the advantage. The spirit refused to remain still for even a moment, twisting its body and using its hands and feet to fight, hitting anything it could reach.

Shane kept the ghost close, not wanting it to take a strong swing or kick. He slipped an arm around the ghost's neck and felt the flesh flake in his grasp as he squeezed to subdue it.

No words came from the ghost's mouth, nor was it at all silent. It screamed and groaned and growled. None of the sounds were intelligible. Everything had a ring of desperation, the sounds and movements alike. It reminded Shane of a cornered animal.

Shane drove a knee into the ghost's body and used his free arm to land blows into its sides, trying to slow it down and get it to at least hold still for a moment. He knew it wouldn't feel pain, but he hoped a sense of self-preservation might slow it down as the ribs in its too-thin body cracked under the force of the blows.

The ghost changed tactics and curled itself into a ball, struggling against Shane's chokehold. As soon as it had made itself small enough, the ghost pushed down with its feet and kicked off, forcing them both into the water.

They rolled over together, splashing through the icy cold water, and the ghost pulled at Shane, dragging him under as they went deeper. He fought to stay above the surface, letting go of the ghost's throat and pushing it away, but it had grasped onto him as firmly as he had once held it. It clung to him like a leech and jerked and spun its body quickly and forcefully.

Shane was pushed under as the ghost got the upper hand and got on top. It forced him below but sank into the water with him, grasping at his face and forcing its burned, bony hands into Shane's mouth.

The freezing water was as black as oil, and Shane struggled against the grip of the burned ghost, forcing it away so he could resurface and breathe. He bit the ghost's hand, chomping through fingers and separating two of them at the knuckle.

CHAPTER 17

IN THE HEART

Losing fingers finally made the ghost recoil, allowing Shane to roll over and then push off, his feet finding purchase on the ground so he could stand and get free of the water.

The light nearly blinded him as he stood. A large picture window facing east and the still-rising sun was right before his eyes. Shane was shin-deep in a bathtub in the middle of a bathroom he hadn't seen before.

The ghost grabbed his legs to pull itself out of the tub, and Shane rained blows on its head, forcing it back into the water. He held it down by the neck and pressed its skull against the porcelain, but the ghost kicked out wildly, hitting Shane in the groin, and knocking him backward out of the tub.

He hit the ground awkwardly, his shoulder crunching into a pile of discarded pizza boxes and causing him to roll to one side. The tub was gone, and he was no longer in the bathroom but one of the bedrooms. The burned ghost was on the floor in front of him, and it came at him again, the transition from one room to another meaning nothing to it.

It jumped and landed on Shane, and the floor cracked and gave way. They fell to the floor below and into a new bedroom. Unlike the others, this one was not cluttered with trash. Instead, a single, small cot had been set against the stone wall, and little else stood out. The floor was concrete like the basement, and there was light from the smallest of windows, up near the ceiling and well out of reach for any normal person.

Shane landed hard on his back and struggled to regain his breath. The ghost was atop him and ready to continue the fight when it suddenly realized where it was. The bloated, white eyes moved though it was a struggle to tell what it was looking at.

The spirit pulled away from Shane and scrambled across the room. It chose the corner opposite the cot and began clawing at the wall as though looking for a hidden door.

The screams of rage had stopped, and now, the ghost whimpered and grunted, digging with ragged fingernails for all it was worth but accomplishing nothing. It soon gave up and scrambled to another portion of the wall, this time focusing on where the wall and floor met, picking at the barest crack in the stone as though its hands were pry bars and it might dig itself free.

Whatever ability a spirit normally had to transition through solid matter, including walls, did not apply in the room. The ghost's hands hit the stone with resounding slaps, the barrier as physical to it as it would have been to Shane.

Shane got to his feet, ready to continue the fight, but it was as if he no longer existed. The ghost ignored him and continued to move about the walls a few inches at a time, looking for a way out.

Shane looked around the room cautiously, not willing to turn his back on the ghost even if it was no longer concerned with him. The cot was lined with a thin blue-and-white-striped mattress, too small for an adult. An olive-drab Army surplus blanket lay atop it. On the blanket was an ancient box of crayons.

There were pictures on the stone wall next to the bed, doodles drawn by crayon in a child's hands. There were stick figures, a yellow sun, what looked like dogs, and trees. Nothing ominous or remarkable at first. But the room had no door, no furnishings, and no sign that whoever was kept there had a way to get free. It was a prison cell as much as it seemed to be a child's room.

Shane followed the line of pictures on the wall, and the scene grew darker as it passed the end of the bed to where the artist would have had to stand and walk around the room. In the drawings, the sun was gone, and there were no trees. There were eyes in shadows, small and cartoonish, and a single stick figure that loomed over the others, rendered all in black.

One of the figures was small but also black, with yellow and orange spikes rising from its head. Shane looked at the ghost still struggling to free itself.

"Is this you?" he asked, pointing to the drawing of the burning stick figure. The ghost did not reply or even look.

Another drawing could have been the skeleton Shane found in the attic. And there was one with yellow hair that could have been Beatrix. It was hard to tell with such simple renderings, but the large, black one remained in each picture.

Mr. Shadow, Shane thought. Who else could it be? And who was the artist?

"Whose room is this?" Shane asked, turning on the frantic ghost.

The spirit was pulling at a small chip in the wall. It stopped as Shane spoke and stayed very still, its face pressed to the stone and hands splayed out like it was trying to blend in with the surface.

"We have to get out of here," it whispered at last. The ghost's voice was soft and feminine, and Shane had not expected it. The extent of the wounds made it impossible to tell what it might have been in life, but it seemed like it should have sounded harsher and angrier.

"Where is 'here'?" Shane asked.

The ghost turned to face him, those bloated, white eyes focused on him.

"Kill me," it said.

Shane's brow furrowed, and he was stumped for a reply.

"Kill me now," the ghost begged, scrambling forward across the room. Shane took a step back, but the ghost did not attack. It cowered at his feet and reached for his hands, grasping them, and pulling them against its head.

"I saw you do it to old Dust and Bones. Kill me, please. Quickly!"

Shane pulled away, pushing the ghost back with a foot.

"What the hell is going on? Where are we?"

The ghost would not answer. Instead, it lowered its gaze, still at Shane's feet, and shook its head repeatedly.

"I didn't do anything wrong," it mumbled softly. "Please don't do this. Please no."

Shane crouched down and grabbed the ghost by the face, lifting it and forcing it to look at him.

"Whose room is this? Who's the child who drew on these walls?"

Before the ghost could answer, light, almost musical laughter of a child came from the walls. The sound came from no specific direction or source.

The ghost moaned in despair, pulling away from Shane and covering its mouth with its hands.

"Please no," it said. "No, no, no."

It scrambled away from Shane again, to the farthest corner from the bed. There, it curled into the fetal position, its legs pulled close to its chest and its hands on the back of its head as it buried its face between its knees. It continued to mutter, denying whatever was happening and begging for it to end.

The light from the small window began to dim and Shane turned in a full circle, looking around the room to make sure nothing was sneaking up behind him. The room grew colder as it grew darker. The sound of the child's laughter came again, closer now, from somewhere near the bed.

The spirit did not sneak up on him. It simply appeared, passing through the wall at the foot of the bed. The ghost was that of a boy of maybe six years. He had blond hair and, unlike the ghost huddled in the corner, he bore no signs of trauma. There was no immediate way for Shane to tell what might have happened to cause the boy's death.

The boy curiously watched the ghost in the corner as though watching an insect. He stood next to Shane, only an arm's length away but otherwise ignoring his presence in favor of the huddled spirit.

Now that he had a better look, Shane saw that the boy was dirty, and he looked thin and small for what Shane assumed was his age. Not as malnourished as the burned ghost, but still like he had not eaten well before he died.

"Do you know Mr. Shadow?" Shane asked.

"'Course I do," the boy answered without looking at him. He spoke with a faint New England accent with a hint of mischief in his voice. Something was oddly familiar about him, but Shane could not put his finger on it. He had never seen him, but something still played at the back of his mind.

"I'm so sorry," the burned ghost whispered, splaying itself on the ground before Shane and the boy. "I'm so, so sorry. Please forgive me. I never would have come here, I swear. I didn't choose this; I would never. You have to believe me."

The ghost's voice was panic and dread, and Shane did not doubt the sincerity of its apology. It was mortified that it had shown up in that room and was terrified of what the boy was going to do.

The ghost of the boy approached the burned spirit, almost skipping as he moved. The burned one flattened itself to the ground, face down and begging forgiveness. The little boy laughed and dangled his foot over the other spirit's head.

Something about the sound and cadence of the laughter triggered something in Shane's memory. It reminded him of Beatrix. The more he looked at the boy, the more he felt that there could be something there. He was very young, but the features were not totally dissimilar. They could have been related. He could have been her child or a sibling. Something linked them.

The laughter had not subsided, but the boy quickly bent over. He drove his hand into the top of the burned spirit's skull, crushing the bone as though wielding a hammer. It was swift and brutally efficient. The ghost burst in an instant. The wave of energy washed over the boy as though little more than a gentle breeze, while it forced Shane back a step when it reached him.

The boy turned to face Shane. Neither spoke; the boy only stared at him for a long moment. Finally, the child came toward him, and Shane prepared to defend himself only to watch the child pass him by and go to the bed. He picked up some of the crayons and moved to the wall, where he began drawing a new picture.

The boy chose a blank spot on the wall just below the image of two stick figures with yellow hair, and the giant, black figure that was present in so much of his art. He began drawing what looked like the burned ghost. Shane watched while he colored a representation of himself with his hand jammed into the other ghost's head. Finally, he included what had to be Shane in the picture.

When the image was finished, the boy picked up a black crayon and continued drawing the large, dark stick figure that was in every other picture. In this representation, the figure was watching Shane, the boy, and the burned ghost from off to the side.

Shane looked across the room. He could see nothing, no shadows that might be hiding an ominous figure, and no sense that there was any other spirit in the room. The house could still have tricks that he didn't understand though.

"Is that Mr. Shadow?" Shane asked.

"Uh-huh," the boy said, drawing the shadowy figure's arms especially long and thick.

"Is he here now?"

"He's everywhere," the boy answered. "Always has been."

CHAPTER 18
FAMILY TIES

Shane stepped away from the boy and approached the wall. He reached out for it, letting his fingers touch the stone. It was no cooler than he expected it to be. He walked, letting his fingers trail across the surface. Nothing jumped out, literally or figuratively. He didn't feel the chill of the dead or see anything move. There was only the boy and his drawing.

"Do you know Beatrix?" Shane asked.

"Uh-huh," the boy said, putting more detail into the burned ghost.

"Does she come here often?"

"No," the boy replied. "And her name isn't really Beatrix."

"Brandy Jean," Shane said. The boy giggled.

"Yeah," he said.

"Who is she?"

"She's my twin sister," the boy said. "But we don't look alike anymore."

"I noticed," Shane said. "How come you're here and she's not?"

The boy stopped drawing and looked over his shoulder at Shane, frowning slightly as he did so.

"I can't leave," he said. "I'm not alive."

He returned to his work and Shane continued around the room, not feeling any sign of another spirit.

"She could take you, couldn't she? I've seen her do that. Transport ghosts from one place to another."

"Not me," the boy replied.

"But she comes to visit you?"

"Sometimes," the boy answered.

He pointed to another of his drawings on the wall, one Shane was certain had not been there when he looked earlier. In this picture, there was a tall, blond stick figure and a shorter, blonder one. They were together, being watched by the large, black figure.

Shane looked across the drawings again. Many of them were not the ones he had seen previously. The images were much darker now, and more horrific. They were all still done in the child's crude hand, but the images showed blood and death and creatures that were not of this world.

The closer the pictures got to the bed, the more the first blond stick figure shrank until it was the same size as the other. In the first image on the wall, the tall, shadowy being was smothering one of the blond figures with its hands.

"Is this you?" Shane asked. "Did Mr. Shadow do this to you?"

"What's your name?" the boy asked.

"My name is Shane. What's yours?"

"Ben," the boy replied. "Benjamin Franklin Talbot Jr. That's my whole name."

"That's a long name," Shane said. "Why did Mr. Shadow do this to you?"

Ben stopped coloring and looked back at Shane again. His expression was one of exasperation, as though Shane should have known better than to even ask.

"'Cuz he was scared of me," he said.

It was not the answer Shane expected. The boy went back to his work, filling in the dark figure of Mr. Shadow in his drawing.

"Why was he scared of you, Ben?"

"'Cuz I can kill him, so he had to kill me first. But then I came back, and he got even more scared," Ben answered. "And now, none of his friends are allowed in my room, or else."

"Or else," Shane repeated.

"Or else," the boy said. He tapped the picture he'd drawn of the burned ghost.

Or else they were destroyed. Shane was not sure he understood the dynamics of what was going on. Mr. Shadow, he thought, was working with Beatrix. But the ghost had also killed her brother when they were still children. And it had done so because it was afraid of the power the boy had. He could do what his sister and Shane could. He could destroy ghosts.

If any of that was true, why would the ghost kill the brother but not the sister? Beatrix was dangerous as well, maybe not as much when she was a child, but she definitely was now. If she was working with Mr. Shadow, whatever he was, Shane couldn't understand why.

Maybe Mr. Shadow was afraid that Beatrix would return the same way Ben had. It was clear from the demonstration the boy provided that he was powerful. He had dispatched the burned ghost with no effort. Maybe Mr. Shadow had not anticipated that Ben would return as a ghost and kept Beatrix alive because she was easier to handle that way. It didn't make much sense to Shane as he mulled over the ideas, but he couldn't think of an angle that did.

Shane looked at the other drawings on the wall, each telling a clumsy story, and nearly all of them involving Mr. Shadow. One of the images showed the blond figure that represented Ben sleeping in the bed as Mr. Shadow crouched on his chest.

Another showed a casket in the ground. There were people above, including the Beatrix figure, and a tombstone. The boy had drawn his funeral. Mr. Shadow was in the ground with him, hovering over the coffin.

Shane paused to inspect one that depicted Mr. Shadow eating someone, a stick figure that Shane had not seen in the other drawings. He couldn't tell who it was supposed to be because half of the figure was missing inside of Mr. Shadows' mouth. The large, black form held it in its hands and chewed off its head.

Shane stared at it for a long moment, the way that Mr. Shadow was crouching, and the size of the figure in its hands that it was eating. It looked familiar, despite being childish and drawn with crayon.

"That's Goya," Shane said. "*Saturn Devouring His Son*."

"It's Mr. Shadow," the boy corrected.

His tone was sharp, but he still didn't turn to look at Shane. Shane did not reply, not wanting to rile the spirit any more than he already had. He was not wrong; however, whether the boy meant it to or not, he had recreated the famous Francisco Goya painting.

Shane looked back across the wall at other images for vague similarities to paintings. The one in which Ben was in the bed with Mr. Shadow on his chest was a recreation of *The Nightmare*. In the original, it was a woman and the thing on her chest was some kind of incubus, but the ghost's layout was the same.

What the hell does that mean? Shane thought. Were the images things that had happened? Or was the boy just recreating things he'd seen? Where would the ghost of a child living in a condemned beach house find classical art for inspiration?

"Can I talk to Mr. Shadow?" Shane asked the boy.

The ghost shrugged, moving on to a new image. Shane watched him drag the crayons up and down on the stone wall. His new picture was of Shane, his arms and legs and head being torn off by shadowy hands in all directions.

"How about you call him out for me?" Shane said.

The boy didn't respond.

"Ben," Shane said, his tone sterner than it had been. The ghost kept drawing.

"Ben!"

"He doesn't come in here!" the boy shouted. "He never comes in here. No one is ever allowed in here."

The boy turned and threw the crayon at Shane. It spun over and over and then hit him harmlessly on the chest before falling to the floor. Shane stared at it. It still looked brand new, and there was no sign that Ben had worn it down with his coloring.

Based on the amount of work on the wall, he had been using these crayons for a long time. They were not real, they were ghostly manifestations, and yet they existed apart from him. They had mass and feeling behind them. Shane bent and picked up the crayon. He felt the texture of the paper that wrapped it, and the stiffness of the wax.

The house must be creating and sustaining the physical illusion of everything. Shane looked around the room again. There was no sign of a door, nor any sign that a door had ever been there. Maybe there had not been. Maybe the room had been designed for Ben so no one would ever come in or out.

"Why am I in this room, Ben?"

"I don't know," the boy replied. "No one's allowed in here."

"Because you won't let them, or Mr. Shadow won't let them?"

"I don't know. I don't let Mr. Shadow's friends in."

"How do you know I'm not his friend?"

"'Cuz you're asking so many dumb questions about him. And you're alive."

"Isn't Beatrix his friend? She's alive."

Ben turned to look at Shane.

"She's not his friend," the ghost answered.

"Why not?"

The boy glowered, clearly annoyed with Shane. The light from the window dimmed almost imperceptibly, and Shane saw that the boy's mood affected the room around them.

"Mr. Shadow let Brandy Jean live," the boy began in a rush. "He would have killed her, too. I know he would have; he told me so. He told her so. He doesn't let anyone live, but he has to let her live. She can go places that he can't go and do things that he can't do. It made sense to let her live. He could have let me live, but he chose me first."

He was clearly angry as he let loose the vague details of what had happened. Shane nodded and tried to look understanding. He didn't want the ghost to get angrier. He wanted to keep Ben talking.

"He uses your sister, then," Shane said.

"She doesn't have to stay in one place like he does. When you're dead, you can't keep going places. I'm not allowed to keep going places. You get stuck to something, and it doesn't ever let you go. And you can try to get away, but you only go so far, and then it pulls you right back. Even Mr. Shadow can't get away, so he has to use Brandy Jean."

"But what does he use her for? Where does he need her to go?"

"All kinds of places. Mr. Shadow sends her all over the world, I think. She goes everywhere. He just wants to hurt people that he can't hurt anymore because he's stuck. But with Brandy Jean, he's not stuck. With her help, he's stronger than he ever was, so he can get revenge on everyone he wants."

"Revenge for what?" Shane asked.

"For everything. For being dead. For being alive. He hates them all."

"Who are they? The people he hates," Shane asked.

"Everyone," Ben answered. "Everyone in the world."

CHAPTER 19

LIFE AND DEATH IN SHADOWS

Shane couldn't tell if the boy was speaking metaphorically or just as he understood things. A spirit like Mr. Shadow, based on Shane's limited knowledge, could very well have been something that had a grudge against all living things. Or maybe Ben just didn't understand the scope of the ghost's desires.

If Mr. Shadow had knowledge of other ghosts, if he was the one who knew about spirits like Cassius, then there was more to him than just a spirit that was stuck in a Rhode Island beach house. Either when he was alive or after he died, he must have been in contact with people who collected ghosts. He knew about that world and his knowledge was at least several decades old.

If he was seeking vengeance, it wasn't against everyone. Or maybe that was just a secondary goal, the evolution of something. But he had a plan and was targeting specific people with Beatrix. Setting up her and the Harvesters, releasing dangerous ghosts, that was all for a reason.

Beatrix seemed so disorganized, though. Not that she was bad at what she did; she accomplished her goals efficiently and ruthlessly. But there seemed to be such little care given to anything after the fact. The spirit in the forest and the one in the cornfield had been abandoned and ignored. It was like she started a plan and then gave up on it every time she found the spirit she was looking for.

It couldn't have been as simple as waiting for another paying customer. What did Mr. Shadow get out of that? If he could point her to the ghosts she was capturing, or even the people she was killing, how come none of it came to a proper conclusion? It was very chaotic. She killed, she caused damage, and then nothing. Then she moved on and did it again somewhere else.

"Why does your sister help him?"

"She loves him," Ben said bitterly. "She loves him more than she ever loved me. She doesn't say it, but I know. I can tell. They think I'm a baby, but I'm not stupid. I know more than they think."

Shane didn't understand what the ghost was getting at. Something was lost in how the ghost explained things. Shane had dealt with Eloise long enough to know that a ghost could look like a child but think like an adult. However, they never fully escaped the mind of a child. There were times when she slipped back into childish behavior, including childish ways of understanding the world. It seemed like Ben was doing the same thing.

"You said they weren't friends, though."

"You don't listen," Ben said. "He said that about me, too. He'd say I don't listen. I don't do what I'm told. And then he'd put his hands in my face, and it was like ice and fire inside of me. He pulled my brains apart, and now you're not listening! Do you want the same done to you?"

The boy shouted, frustrated and angry, and Shane put his hands up in a placating manner.

"I'm listening," he said.

"She's not his friend; that's what I said. But he is her friend. Or she wants him to be. But he doesn't like anyone. Mr. Shadow can't like anything. Brandy Jean wants everyone to like her. She always needs to be special. She needs all the attention."

It took some effort for Shane not to scoff. The boy had obviously not spent much time with his sister out in the world. She did not want everyone to like her. He could buy the bit about her needing attention, though. She did like to make a scene.

"So, Brandy Jean likes Mr. Shadow? But why, if he hurt you?"

Ben's hands balled into fists, and the house shuddered. The window that was set high into the wall vanished as the stone grew over it like frost spreading. There was still light, some kind of ambient illumination that came from nowhere specific, but the room was much darker.

"Because she's stupid! I told her not to trust him, and she said I was just a kid. I don't understand. I understand everything. I understand everything! She'll regret trusting him. I know she will."

Ben screamed the final words, and the house rumbled. Shane felt the floor moving under his feet in a way that was hard to explain. It wasn't rotating; it was moving like it was a living thing. The floor, the walls, and even the ceiling were flowing, moving like something fluid yet solid at the same time.

Shane felt the floor rise and then lower in a smooth, rolling motion. Cold air rolled off the boy in waves, and Shane realized what the movement under his feet reminded him of. Muscle and bone under flesh. The house was moving like it was alive.

"I hear you," Shane said. "I have issues with Brandy Jean, too. But I need to find her. Can you help me?"

The darkness deepened, and so did the cold. The shape of the room was different now. It had grown larger, the walls had pulled away, and now, Shane couldn't even see the ones to his left and right. Ahead of him, behind the boy, the drawings on the wall moved slowly. The figures walked or crawled across the stone, their little, simple faces watching Shane with eyes that glowed faintly from the shadows.

"Why do you want to find Brandy Jean?" the boy asked.

"I need her stopped," Shane said. "She's been letting a lot of ghosts loose and causing a lot of trouble. I need to make sure she's not going to hurt anyone again."

The darkness swallowed the wall, covering the crayon images save for the eyes, which shone like pinpricks of light. It crept up on the boy and covered him like a cloak, oozing over his shoulders and arms and across the top of his head.

"Are *you* her friend?" the boy asked. The darkness closed over him almost totally. His face was visible, cast in shadow but leaving just enough exposed to show his eyes, nose, and mouth.

Shane paused before answering. What did the boy want to hear? His reaction to his sister seemed to waver between love and hate. Did he want to save her from Mr. Shadow? Or was he condemning her for choosing Mr. Shadow over him?

"I'm trying to be her friend," Shane said.

Ben smiled and the darkness of the room swallowed his face. The points of light behind him, the tiny eyes of his stick figure army, blinked and moved. They shuffled about in the dark, spreading out to surround Shane. They moved away from the walls, no longer bound by two dimensions. They were real now, independent and free to roam as they pleased.

"Then you are Mr. Shadow's friend," the boy's voice said. "And his friends aren't allowed in here."

Shane cursed in his head. He had a fifty-fifty chance of getting that one right, and he messed up.

The boy was just a shadow on the wall. The light from the eyes of his drawings was too faint and too scattered to offer enough illumination. Shane walked back toward a wall but found nothing solid behind him. Then movement from the corner of his eye caught his attention.

Shane did not see the first attack coming. The boy came at him from behind. Something hit Shane in the back, and he felt a sharp pain stab into his kidney. His teeth clenched involuntarily, and a strained growl escaped from his lips as his back spasmed, and he fell to his knees.

The blow felt like he had been shot, just a point of fiery pain that sank into his flesh and radiated throughout his body. Ben came at him again when he was on his knees and Shane caught a glimpse this time, a quick view of the boy's hand as it snapped out and sank right into Shane's flesh, passing through his chest and crunching against ribs.

His lung compressed like it had been squeezed, and he gasped to draw in air. Shane fell forward, using one hand to hold himself up while he drew in as much air as he could. He saw the boy coming for him again and lashed out, backhanding Ben across the side of the face and knocking him backward.

The floor rolled violently like waves in the ocean, and Shane was lifted and tossed backward. He landed on his back as the building rumbled. He stood up awkwardly, struggling to keep his footing on the stone that moved like jelly beneath him.

Ben ran at him, yelling in a childish rage. Shane had more time to prepare and avoided the boy's attack easily, kicking him in the leg to knock him down as he sidestepped the assault.

The floor surged again, dropping out from under Shane and then coming back up swiftly. Shane slammed into the floor and found himself being rolled to one side as it flipped and went from horizontal to nearly vertical.

He tumbled endlessly, with no wall in sight to stop his fall. The tiny lights of the drawings swirled around him as though they were falling as well, and he reached out, struggling to find something to grab onto. There was nothing but the smooth, cold stone of the floor.

Shane reached a hand into his pocket, bouncing against the floor as he rolled downward. He needed to get away from the boy and hopefully get the house to settle down long enough for him to get on his feet.

His fingers felt cold iron in his pocket, and he slipped one into the iron ring there. Moments later, he heard an angry yell from the boy again as he appeared from the darkness, unaffected by the floor that was now a vertical surface. He came at Shane, swooping through the shadows like a bird.

Shane's fist made contact with the boy's face. The iron ring touched Ben's jaw, and he vanished. Shane had no idea where the boy's haunted item was or how far he'd been transported when the iron connected with his flesh, but any respite Shane could get was welcome.

Shane slammed into a wall as soon as the boy vanished. The house had reorganized itself, and it sounded like every board was warping at once, every stone was cracking, and every window was breaking. It was a cacophony of destruction, a deafening racket that made it seem like the house was collapsing.

Shane got to his feet, and he was not in the stone room any longer. He was in one of the upstairs bedrooms, but the walls were breaking as though great pressure was being forced down upon them. Wood splintered and flew at Shane. He raised his arms to cover his face and fell, landing in the dining room at the head of the table.

The table collapsed, and Shane scuttled back to avoid the ceiling or anything from the upstairs bedroom landing on him. His hands and feet dropped out from under him, and he fell with a splash into the pool in the basement. He was there for only an instant, long enough to lift his head, and then he was in the living room, looking out the large picture window at a moonlit night over the ocean.

Waves crashed violently against the house, smashing through the sliding glass door, and flooding the room. The force knocked Shane back into a hutch. He fell through it and was in the bathroom, rising from the bathtub.

He was unable to stay rooted for more than a few seconds. The house continued to heave and surge violently. Every time it threw him somewhere, he found himself in another room. Some he had visited before, some he had not.

The effect was disorienting, and it was hard to know where he should move, or even where he should stand before he found himself somewhere else with new features and a new landscape.

As Shane struggled to stay in one place, upright and secure, the only consistency around him was the ever-increasing destruction. As the rooms continued to change, they were falling apart under the stress of the shifts.

All the glass he could see was broken, and all the walls were cracked and crumbling. If the house kept moving as it was, it seemed like it would break itself to pieces with Shane inside.

Shane moved toward the exits when he saw them. Windows, doors, anything that looked like it might be a way out. Sometimes the effort was wasted, and he found himself in a new room, farther from any exit than he had been, but he continued. He needed to take whatever control he could, to go where he wanted rather than where the house wanted him.

Drywall shattered and sprayed Shane with dust. Support beams fell from the walls, and the ceiling above came down, swinging toward him and nearly hitting him. From the living room, Shane ran toward the front door.

He needed to escape before the house swallowed him in its destruction.

CHAPTER 20

AT THE END OF TIME

The floor broke, and Shane was back in the boy's dark room in the basement. He made a run for the window, and he was in the dining room. He hit the ground running each time, not bothering to look around to see what was happening, just going toward what he knew was the closest way out.

Something squealed within the walls, and Shane couldn't tell if it was mechanical or living or something else. It sounded almost like metal stress, but other times like a trapped animal. He tumbled through a hole in the floor and found himself in the front hallway. The front door was a short distance in front of him, and he scrambled forward, grabbing the doorknob and pulling it open.

The house heaved, and he went through the door. But he was not outside as he had expected. Instead, he was tumbling down a staircase. Except as he went down, he saw the night sky, and the living room, and the basement, and the dining room. The house spun around him, and he was no longer going down, he was going up.

Everything seemed to merge at one time. Water splashed over him, but he continued to fall down the stairs, out of the pool, and into something else. He put his hands out and tried to stop his progress, but he was moving up and not down. Gravity pulled him the wrong way, ripping his fingers from the steps and tossing him up once more.

The stairs came to an end, and Shane was in the attic, face-down on the dusty floor while the wooden walls cracked and fell apart around him. Ben was there, too, standing where the skeleton ghost had been the first time Shane was in the room.

"Not fair!" the boy yelled.

He came for Shane again, attacking his face this time. Shane fell back and extended a foot, using the boy's momentum to lift him as he raised a fist and punched him in the face. The iron of the ring connected again, and Ben vanished.

Like before, the house reacted violently to the attack on the ghost. The attic floor dropped out and water rose. The room became a mishmash of the attic and the basement.

Water splashed and Shane turned, but too slowly this time. Ben was behind him, and he lashed out, hitting Shane in the chest. The blow felt like a knife blade slashing across muscle. The force, however, was otherworldly. Shane flew backward, breaking through walls one after another, each one painfully slamming muscle and bone, until he landed in the living room.

Shane lay there in a heap, struggling to breathe and push the pain from his mind. He had passed through no fewer than three walls, each one collapsing under his weight. He felt as though he'd been hit by a car.

The noise of the house was nearly deafening. Breaking, cracking, and crumbling sounded all around him. Shane tried to sit up, to see where Ben was, and if he was attacking again. His muscles wouldn't respond.

A shadow passed before his eyes, and the ghost was there again. He stared down at Shane, anger twisting his features as he grabbed Shane by the shirt, lifting him like he was nothing.

"You're not allowed to be here," Ben hissed.

The boy tossed Shane to the side and sent him flying. Shane crashed through the sliding glass door and careened out over the wraparound porch. He landed with a soft thud in damp sand some fifteen feet from the door. The softness of the sand had blissfully cushioned the fall and he sat up, wincing with pain and praying to avoid another attack.

There was no noise save for the waves lapping gently at the shore behind him. The air was cool, and the briny smell was strong. He was not thrust into another room or spun about like a rag doll. Ben had thrown him from the house. Shane was outside now, free from the house and the madness of its structure.

Ben stormed out of the living room, through the broken door, and came down onto the beach. Shane was on his feet as quickly as he could stand, ready to meet him.

"You don't belong here!" the boy yelled.

He came at Shane swinging. His rage was bordering on a tantrum now, and he fought as such. His attacks were wild and childish, swinging haphazardly in hopes of doing as much random damage as possible.

Shane caught the boy's wrist as he windmilled his arms and jerked Ben forward then to the side quickly to throw him off-balance. He forced the ghost down onto the sand, pushing him face-first into it to subdue him. Ben kicked and twisted, and Shane was forced to bend one of his arms back in a submission hold.

Ben screamed, just angry yelling at first, and then threats. Shane pushed his arm back even farther to get him to calm down.

"I will break your arm," Shane warned.

"I'll break you," the ghost replied.

He bucked and fought despite the pressure Shane put on his arm, twisted as far behind the boy's back as he could get it. His erratic movements caused the shoulder joint to pop, and Shane felt it dislocate in his hands.

Ben shrieked and continued to fight. He thrashed so violently that the ghostly flesh of his upper arm tore, and Shane pulled the arm off the ghost's body. It disintegrated in his hands and vanished, which only further enraged the child.

"It's not fair," Ben screamed.

"Get used to it," Shane replied.

The ghost seemed to calm at that, realizing the futility in fighting now that he'd lost an arm and Shane was not about to give up. Kneeling on the boy's back to keep him in place, Shane took a moment to catch his breath and consider his next move.

The sound of the water lapping at the shore continued to grow closer. Shane and the ghost were on the small expanse of beach between the porch and the ocean, and he knew it wouldn't be long before the tide came in and covered the area. He needed to decide what to do with the boy and soon.

The smart move was to destroy him. However, if the boy was opposed to Beatrix and Mr. Shadow, he could have useful information if Shane could calm him down enough to talk.

He was still considering his options when a quick burst of freezing air preceded something slamming hard into his back. Shane was knocked off of Ben and tossed into the wet sand. He felt chilly claws digging into his flesh and bit back a scream of pain and anger.

Shane grabbed at whatever he could, taking hold of cold, rubbery flesh and bone as he rolled his attacker over with him in the wet sand, fighting it off and getting his bearings.

A half-flayed face stared back at Shane as he got on top of the thinly muscled body of his attacker. Bloodshot eyes looked into his own, but from the nose down, the skin had been peeled away, revealing a skeleton's nose and lipless mouth. The flesh had been perfectly excised all around the skull, front and back, leaving only the top half.

Broken arms and legs bent at impossible angles and tried to overpower Shane. It was another of Beatrix's Hounds. Shane acted quickly, breaking the fingers on its right hand, but backed off as movement from the corner of his eye alerted him to a second broken spirit closing in.

Shane pushed the ghost away and got to his feet. The Hound scrambled up on all fours while another crept closer from the porch of the house. Two more were behind it, and another came from Shane's other side.

He cursed softly, watching five of the twisted monstrosities close in on him like hyenas approaching prey. Each ambled forward on shaky, broken limbs. Their bodies displayed different cruelties, with bones broken in unexpected ways.

Like the others Shane had fought, each of the Hounds had been partially skinned, but only on the skull. One had inch-wide strips pulled away around its face, while another had a perfect triangle carving that started between its eyes and continued down to below its mouth. The exposed skulls were always clean and polished, and the cuts were perfectly straight and surgical in nature.

Ben was on his feet, with his one remaining hand balled into a fist and an angry scowl on his face. Shane knew he had no hope of defeating the boy plus five of his sister's Hounds. The fight would be over before it started, especially in his already weakened condition.

He began backing toward the sea. If they were going to attack him, they should at least work for it. He felt the water rushing over his boots, and then up his calves as he continued to retreat. The Hounds moved as a group, with no communication between them but each of them acting as if they'd had it all planned.

Someone else stood watching off the side of the porch. It was not Beatrix as Shane had expected, but Lanthimos. He stood alone, his eyes locked on Shane as the disfigured ghosts followed him onto the surf.

Ben screamed another wordless expression of rage and stomped into the water. It was not Shane he came for, though, it was the Hounds.

"You're not allowed to be here," the boy shouted. He reached the first spirit and slammed his good hand onto the top of its head.

The Hound's body exploded instantly. The spiritual matter that had created it faded to motes of dust and vanished as the energy rushed out in all directions. It knocked the other Hounds over while the boy seemed to revel in it as it washed over him.

The Hounds turned on Ben then, too beast-like to know which threat was their true target. From the house, Lanthimos shouted for them to stop, his words barely reaching Shane's ear.

The next Hound came for Ben and the boy drove his hand through its face, causing the ghost to explode and knock the next one down. Ben didn't even allow that one to get to its feet before he repeated the destruction, breaking it apart with a single blow.

Shane had never seen a ghost fight like the boy. It had to be something to do with the abilities he had when he was alive, the ability to see and fight ghosts the way Shane and Beatrix could. Some of that power had carried over and evolved in death to make him dangerous to both the living and the dead.

Maybe the reason Beatrix and Mr. Shadow had left Ben in the basement of the house was because there was nothing they could do with him. Unless Mr. Shadow was remarkably powerful as well, it seemed likely that Ben could have destroyed him as easily as he destroyed the Hounds.

The two remaining Hounds were smarter in their approach. They left Shane entirely, recognizing Ben as the greater threat, even as Lanthimos brought them to heel and stay on target.

They rushed the boy as one, coming from both sides. With only one hand, Ben could not fight two at once. He still thought and fought like a child and could not work defense.

One of the Hounds subdued his arm, holding the ghost steady while the other began to assault him. As strong as Ben was, he still had the weaknesses of any normal ghost. Their claws tore through his body and shredded him, pulling off pieces as he screamed and kicked and fought them off.

Shane approached from the water. It might have been a dumb idea, but he realized that he would have to contend with whoever won. Better the one who still thought like a human.

He pulled one of the Hounds off Ben, wrapping an arm around its throat and squeezing as he dragged it away. He inserted the fingers from his free hand into the empty skeletal eye sockets and pulled off the top of the spirit's head, falling back and using his weight as leverage to bust its head open.

The Hound exploded and Shane groaned in pain, taking a moment to catch his breath. Ben turned on the final Hound and punched it in the face. It exploded as well, the force knocking Shane back one more time. He lay on the shore, water cascading across his face as he sputtered and struggled to sit up.

Ben was crouched in front of him as he finally righted himself. They looked at one another and Shane thought, for a moment, there might be an understanding.

"Why did you help me?" the boy asked.

"Because those things would have destroyed you," Shane replied.

Ben smiled and then laughed.

"You're stupid. Now I'm going to kill you."

CHAPTER 21

SPIRALING DOWN TO OBLIVION

Ben lunged, his one arm extending clumsily. Shane swatted the attack aside easily and launched himself at the ghost. There was no negotiating or working with him. He was too much like his sister, too unpredictable, and too dangerous. If he had valuable information, Shane would never get it.

He took hold of the boy's arm, preventing another of his painful attacks, and dragged him to the ground.

"I'm gonna kill you!" the boy shouted again.

Shane said nothing. He took the ghost by the back of the head and began to squeeze. Ben struggled and fought as Shane got him face-down in the sand.

As much sympathy as Shane had for what the boy had endured, for losing his sister and being imprisoned in the house, he was too dangerous and unstable. He reminded Shane of Vivienne in some ways, just fueled by anger and a need to hurt. He couldn't be allowed to continue.

Shane pushed with both hands. He heard someone scream just as the ghost's skull began to crack.

On the far side of the beach, behind Lanthimos, Beatrix was already running toward him. Ben's skull collapsed, and the boy's body exploded just as he locked eyes with her.

Shane felt a chill settling into his fingertips that raced up his hands and through his wrists as though he had dipped his arms into a freezing lake. Ben's body came apart in a fierce blast of energy so powerful that Shane was lifted high into the air and tossed backward.

Beatrix, still yards away, was knocked over as well, and Shane landed hard in the weed-filled sand next to the house, twenty feet from where he started. The ground was soft enough to do little damage, though the force of falling was enough to stun him.

The house rumbled next to him and planks of siding and the gutters fell away. Shane could hear more crumbling on the inside, reacting to the boy's destruction. He was not sure how the house and Ben had become so closely integrated, but clearly, it was held together at least in part by the ghost's power.

As Shane tried to get back to his feet, a leather boot clipped him in the side of the face, loosening a tooth and sending him reeling.

"I've never met anyone who wanted me to kill them as much as you," Beatrix said, kneeling on his neck. Her nose was bleeding, and the hair on the unshaven side of her head was disheveled. Her eyes were wild and full of hate. Behind her, Lanthimos stared down at Shane as well.

Shane couldn't speak to give a response. The pressure from her knee cut off his ability to breathe and was causing his head to swim. He tried to draw in air, but she wasn't allowing it. Her fist hit him square in the face as she rained blows again and again, breaking his nose, until he could feel blood pooling around his eye sockets.

"You're going to wish it was as easy as being dead," she said, laughing at him. "You're going to wish you took a goddamn toaster into the bathtub this morning, Solo."

Shane reached out and attempted to push her away. Lanthimos circled and kicked him in the side of the head.

Beatrix got to her feet, and they worked in tandem, beating Shane as he lay in the sand. Boots collided with his gut, chest, neck, face, and anywhere else they could make contact. He was spitting up blood and gasping for air when Beatrix told Lanthimos to stop.

Shane was dizzy and disoriented. Every inch of him felt pain, but he was relieved that the beating had stopped, even if only momentarily. Someone grabbed his wrist and he felt himself being dragged through the sand.

He was in too much pain, too sore and exhausted, to fight back. He allowed them to move him because it meant they weren't causing any damage. It was a moment to catch his breath and clear his head.

Sand changed to something harder beneath Shane's back. He was being dragged onto the wraparound porch, across the broken glass, and into the living room of the house.

He could see Beatrix pulling him with Lanthimos at her side. The house was in shambles. The rooms were irregularly shaped: The strange transitioning it had undergone had altered the structure. Beatrix pulled him over impossible bulges in the wood and through a doorway into the room her brother had been in, now accessible from the main floor.

"I want you to see this," she said, tossing Shane to the cold, stone floor and lifting him by the back of his shirt so he could see the wall.

Beatrix crouched next to Shane, her fist twisted in the back of his shirt so she could hold him up. She pointed toward the stone wall and the series of crayon drawings her brother had made.

"Look at them," she ordered.

Some of the images were the same ones Shane had seen, but others had not been there before. Two blond children, Brandy Jean and Ben, confronted by the dark figure called Mr. Shadow. The image of Ben in the ground with his sister at his funeral was there, but there were more between. Images of Mr. Shadow watching the children, the children running from him, and even fighting him from the looks of things.

"I'm here because of my brother," she said. "You see?"

She pointed to a drawing of Ben between her and Mr. Shadow.

"He was going to kill us. Consume us. But Ben fought for me. He was just like me. We were the same, and he sacrificed himself. And Mr. Shadow spared us because of that. Because he saw that power in us, and the goodness in Ben. He could have consumed us both, but he didn't. He did not destroy Ben's ghost and let him stay here. And he spared me. He did that for us. And you just undid it!"

Shane scoffed, blood running from a half-dozen places on his face.

"Not how he told it," he said.

Her hands twisted harder into his collar, and she pulled Shane closer to her face.

"You just don't know when to shut up, do you?"

"God, I've been thinking the same about you since we met," he replied, choking out the words.

She punched him again and lifted his head higher.

"Look! Look at us. We were inseparable. We were the same soul. Do you know what that means, Solo? We were the same, him and me. He was where I kept all the good parts of myself. And you just destroyed him."

She got into his face then, nearly nose to nose, staring at him intently.

"Ben was the one who convinced me I needed to listen to Shadow. To survive, I needed to get rid of all those good parts and let him hold them. And now that's gone. Thanks to you."

Shane smiled, blood seeping between his teeth and over his lips.

"Well, ain't that a bitch," he said.

She smiled back, a manic expression as her eyes searched his face for something only she could see.

"You're going to feel so much pain, Solo. And it's going to last forever. This house has held the dead for so long, they're a part of it. They're woven into the walls; you can't pull them apart. Look what happened when you destroyed Ben. The house needs the ghosts, and the ghosts need the house. But they'll work on you for as long as they can. You're never going to leave."

"Put me in prison like Ben, huh?" Shane asked.

She squeezed his face, and he was certain she'd start beating him again, but she did not.

"You'd be better served begging for death than baiting me," she advised.

Shane chuckled despite the pain. He wouldn't beg, and she wouldn't show mercy. Something came to mind as he stared her in the eyes.

"I noticed you were late to the party. You didn't come with Lanthimos, did you?"

The other man was not in the room. Shane didn't know where she'd left him, but he was sure she hadn't arrived with him. She would have stopped the fight with Ben earlier, and she would never have let the Hounds attack him as they had.

"I want to introduce you to the other spirits in the house, Solo. I think you're going to get a real kick out of them. Mr. Shadow and I left a lot of them here. They've been lonesome for a long time."

"As long as it's not Bones up in the attic or Ashy down in the basement. Had a run at them already," he said.

Her expression was unreadable as she dragged Shane onto the bed and knelt on his throat again.

"You're going to have to wait and see, I guess," she replied.

"Know who didn't wait? Your buddy, Lanthimos, when he sent your Hounds after me. Except they seemed to have a real taste for your brother," Shane croaked.

Beatrix pulled something up from the side of the bed and paused, looking at him.

"You're not getting out of this with words, Solo."

She fastened a leather restraint to his wrist and then repositioned herself, doing the same to his other wrist. Shane spit blood against the wall and sighed.

"Sure, sure. Just don't be shocked if you look for those freak ghosts and come up five short."

Beatrix pulled the restraints tight, ensuring that Shane had no room to wriggle free or get any leverage. She stood up, looked down at him, and smiled broadly.

"Now *this* is a great look," she said. "Can't wait to see you in a month or two."

She turned her back on Shane then and took a few steps toward a door that had not been in the room before. She paused, looked up at the broken ceiling, and then put her hand on the door frame.

"This one is yours," she said. "You have to keep him alive. You can do whatever with him, but you keep him alive. Or Mr. Shadow will hear about it. You understand?"

The house lurched and debris fell from the ceiling, scattering across the floor at her feet. She patted the wall and nodded.

"Make sure he lives," she said again.

She left without another word.

The restraints on Shane's wrist were wide and well-made, and she had affixed them tightly. No matter how he moved, he couldn't even pull his hands down even an inch. He was stuck at the mercy of whatever waited in the shadows.

CHAPTER 22

BOUND

Shane lay still on the dirty, old bed, staring at the cracked stone ceiling above him. As the adrenaline wore off, the pain in his body increased. His head throbbed, and he couldn't breathe through his nose. He felt the blood drying around his eyes, making it awkward to blink. There were aches throughout his face, chest, arms, and legs. He must have had broken bones, but he was too exhausted and too sore all over to assess which ones were badly damaged and which ones were just horribly bruised.

The faint light in the room never changed, and Shane lost track of time. It might have been an hour or several when he heard footsteps approach. He turned, blinking away the dried blood around his eyes, and saw Lanthimos at his bedside.

"Are you the dumbest man alive or do you just like getting your ass kicked?" he asked.

"I don't think you're winning a contest of smarts here," Shane replied. "You think she's not going to find out what you did?"

"What did I do?" Lanthimos asked.

"She didn't know you came here. She was too pissed at me to care that you were here at all. But she's going to go looking for those Hounds of yours, and when she does, they're going to be gone. I'm guessing it's not easy to replace five of them."

"What makes you think she didn't know?"

"Because if it was her, they would have only attacked me."

"Doesn't matter," Lanthimos replied. "You destroyed her brother before she saw what they had done to him, anyway. Even if she asks, I can say they attacked you. That was the intent, anyway."

Shane laughed and shook his head.

"I see why she's the boss, even though she's a few cherries short of a sundae. She at least knows how to handle a job. You got too greedy, Adrian."

"You have no idea what you're talking about."

"Greedy, greedy, greedy," Shane said, grinning. "You could have gotten away with one. Maybe even two. But five? How dumb do you think Beatrix is? You think she's going to believe I took out all five in the condition I was in? No way."

"We'll see," Lanthimos said.

"Yes, we will."

He was goading Lanthimos, baiting him to get a reaction, but Shane wasn't lying. Five Hounds plus her brother. Beatrix had to know how formidable a power Ben was on his own. When she thought about it, she'd realize something had happened that wasn't supposed to. She'd realize Lanthimos had betrayed her.

Even if Beatrix realized what Lanthimos had done, Shane would still be tied to a bed in the house. He needed to do something more to get himself free.

The other man left the room and Shane struggled against his bonds. The leather cuffs were strong and left no room for movement. No matter how Shane twisted or jerked his arms free, he made no progress.

Something clicked under the bed. Shane held still and listened until the sound came again, a sharp, crisp click like the snapping of fingers. Lanthimos was gone from the room and maybe the house. Whatever he or Beatrix had left Shane with was making itself known.

"You plan on just staying down there?" Shane asked.

The finger snap sound came again, twice in quick succession. As the seconds passed, he stayed still and listened carefully. The click came again, and it had moved closer to his head but was still under the bed. He felt a pulling at his right side and turned to see the tips of four fingers pressing into the mattress, just enough to jostle him.

Shane watched as the hands got a better grip and began to pull. The fingertips were pale, and the nails were broken and encrusted with dirt. The ghost slowly pulled itself up until its face crept over the edge of the bed. Thin strands of black hair hung over a pale face. Eyes the color of mud stared into Shane's as the ghost pulled itself level with him.

It was an older woman with sagging, bloated flesh that was pale as paste. Her lips were cracked, and there was blood crusted around her nostrils and in the corners of her eyes. She stayed low, her chin resting on the mattress, and stared at Shane.

"You want to help me out of this?" he said.

She began to reach over, and for a second, Shane thought she might be trying to free him. His opinion quickly changed when her clammy, damp hands crossed over his face and settled above his mouth. She pressed down, squeezing his nostrils shut and covering his lips at the same time.

Shane tried to shake her off, but she held firm. The pain from his nose was blistering. Her palm over his mouth formed a seal, and he couldn't draw air. Even as he shook his head side to side and up and down, her grip held on.

The ghost grinned wildly watching him struggle. Thirty seconds became a minute, and his chest began to hurt. A minute became a minute and a half, and he started to feel as though his chest might burst. The damage to his nose in the beating he received had made breathing difficult to begin with.

Spots danced before his eyes and, just as he felt like he might pass out, the ghost released him, holding her hand just above his face and watching with a delighted expression as he gulped in some air. She let him take just two breaths and then replaced her hand, forcing him to endure the same process all over again.

Over and over, the torture played out. Shane could not get as much air as he needed with each brief break, and each time, the sensation of losing consciousness came to him faster. Finally, when it seemed like he would not make it to his next breath, she pulled her hand away.

She slipped away without a word, hiding under the bed again as Shane breathed deeply, filling his lungs while he had the chance.

Rest lasted only a moment. As Shane drew deep breaths, his eyes focused on the cracked, dirty ceiling above him. The water stains across the stone organized themselves into a shape before his eyes. It looked almost like the outline of a person until it moved. It was not a person, but another ghost staring down at him.

The spirit had dark skin and dark hair. It grinned at him with cracked, stained teeth, and began to crawl across the ceiling. It was upside-down as it moved in a crab walk. It kept its eyes locked on Shane even as it bent backward to move from ceiling to wall and climb down headfirst.

"Such a gift," the ghost whispered cheerfully. "Such a joy!"

The spirit released the wall and fell onto the bed, twisting its body so it was on its hands and knees, straddling Shane and looking into his face. The ghost smelled of mud and mold, like things forgotten in a basement. Yellowed eyes searched his face, and it touched him, running gritty, cold fingertips across Shane's cheeks and lips.

"Such a delight," it whispered, nuzzling into his cheek.

Shane struggled to get away from the ghost, but the restraints held fast, and all he could do was turn his head as the ghost buried its face in his neck. He felt the cold flesh and colder breath on him, he felt the lips trailing across his collarbone and up his neck to just beneath his ear. His body went stiff as he felt the broken teeth begin to nip at him, taking small, gentle bites.

The ghost made soft, rodent-like noises as it began to bite harder, nibbling up and down Shane's neck until it was sinking its teeth in. It gnawed on him and pierced the flesh, taking a piece from his shoulder where it met his neck and causing him to scream and jerk his body.

"I can't taste it anymore," the ghost said sadly, pulling away so that it looked down into his face again. Shane could see his blood on the ghost's lips as it chewed a mouthful of his flesh. "I can't taste it!"

The ghost wailed in sadness and Shane jerked his head forward, smashing his forehead into the ghost's mouth as hard as he could.

The ghost cried out as its front teeth collapsed into its mouth, and it pulled away from him, covering its bloody lips with one hand. It looked pained and offended by Shane's actions.

"Not a gift!" it spat. "Filthy thing."

The ghost reached for his throat but the pale spirit under the bed reappeared, grasping the other's wrists. She shook her head and the ghost straddling Shane hissed and pulled itself free.

"Not going to kill," the ghost growled. "Just punish."

The pale one released it, and the ghost on top fixed its yellow eyes back on Shane.

"Punish," the ghost repeated.

It pushed its fingers into Shane's mouth. They were cold and spongy and tasted sour and old. He jerked his head away, but the ghost moved with him. The fingertips wriggled across his tongue to the back of his throat, and Shane bit down hard before they could plunge any deeper and trigger a gag reflex to make him vomit.

The ghost screeched and tried to pull away, but Shane's bite was firm as he continued to apply pressure. The struggling made it worse, and the ghost's hand eventually snapped back, two fingers missing and fading to nothing in Shane's mouth.

The taste vanished with the fingers, but Shane spat anyway. He prepared for another assault when Lanthimos entered the room.

"What the hell are you doing in here?" he demanded.

The ghost atop Shane scuttled back to the wall, crawling away in disappointment, watching the living men as it faded into a shadow.

"Making friends," Shane answered.

"You better watch yourself," Lanthimos warned. "There are more ghosts than just Spider in here. She can keep you in here for days. Weeks, even. They'll all have a go at you, and she won't care as long as they leave you alive."

"Unless someone lets me out," Shane suggested.

Lanthimos laughed and shook his head.

"You just don't know when you've lost, do you?"

"Do you?" Shane asked. "Why did you come here alone with those Hounds? My guess is she's slipping. Maybe things were a little chaotic at first, but now they're a lot more chaotic? Having a hard time making things work the way you expect them to? This was all about money once, right? But if she's just killing everyone and none of your hunts are working out, who's paying your bills?"

"You have no idea what you're talking about," Lanthimos replied.

"Yes, I do. I destroyed your swamp ghost, the scarecrow, the creep in the woods, and Cassius. Those were all paydays; now they're not. So, what's the mission of the Harvesters? Watch Beatrix lose her mind in real time then clean up her messes?"

"She's saved my life more times than I can count. If you think you're driving a wedge between us, you're crazier than you look."

"I didn't make you come here without her. I never made those ghosts attack her brother. *You* did that," Shane said.

They stared at each other, and Shane could see the conflict on Lanthimos' face. Even if he didn't want to admit it to Shane, he was having a hard time denying it to himself. Shane was right; there was a fracture between them. There was no way Beatrix was a reliable partner.

"She sacrificed her brother to Mr. Shadow. She may not tell it that way, but that's what the kid told me. That's why no one was allowed in this damn house. He didn't trust her or anyone she sent here. You think she's going to have your back when she finds out you sent those ghosts and they tore him up? That you went behind her back to get me?"

"We've been partners for years," Lanthimos countered.

"Her brother was her twin," Shane replied. "And she still works for the thing that killed him."

"You're going to die, Ryan. Make peace with it," Lanthimos said.

"Have you?" Shane said. "You've got a better shot at living with me. Either I'll kill her myself, or I'll slow her down long enough for you to get away. But you're not reaching the end of this in one piece once she gets her head on straight and looks for those Hounds."

Lanthimos stared at him. Shane could see the gears turning. The house sensed something as well, and the already damaged structure creaked, loosening dust and rubble.

The pale ghost emerged from under the bed, creeping out slowly as she lifted a swollen hand to point a spindly finger at Lanthimos.

"No," the ghost whispered. "No!"

"Excuse me?" Lanthimos said bitterly. "Are you giving me orders?"

The ghost hesitated briefly but then, emboldened by some idea that she was on the correct path, she crawled forward.

"You leave this place or die!"

CHAPTER 23

UNBOUND

If Lanthimos was intimidated by the ghost, he gave no sign of it. Instead, he waited for it to approach him and then reached behind his back, retrieving one of the tablet devices Shane had seen the Harvesters use when hunting Cassius.

He tapped a button, and an electrical discharge hit the ghost, causing it to collapse. It had done little to Cassius, but weaker spirits were stunned by the device, and it allowed Lanthimos to approach the now-incapacitated ghost and kneel next to it.

"You are a dog. You heel, you roll over, and you play dead. If you bite, you get put down. Don't forget it," he said softly.

The ghost made no sound and didn't move. Lanthimos watched it silently for a moment and then got to his feet, searching the ceiling for the other ghost.

"Your job is to do what we tell you to do. If I tell you to shut up, you shut up. If I tell you to bury yourself in the sand, you bury yourself in the goddamn sand. Nothing more! I am in charge. Do you understand? I am in charge!"

He shouted the final words, and it seemed like he was saying them more to himself than the spirits.

Lanthimos looked at Shane and clenched his jaw. He slipped the device behind his back and approached the bed, stripping off the leather cuffs that held Shane in place.

"You're not as right as you think you are," the man said.

"Then why help me?" Shane asked, sitting up.

"Because you're not totally wrong either. This is the only help you'll get from me. If I see you again, I'll kill you myself."

They stared at each other for a moment until Lanthimos stepped back and Shane got to his feet.

"Fair enough," he replied. "You'll never see me again."

He struck out with his elbow and forearm, clipping Lanthimos across the jaw and knocking him to his knees. The house roared and trembled that chunks of the stone ceiling fell free and shattered on the ground.

Shane slipped an arm around Lanthimos' throat. The man had nearly killed him three times and had been at Beatrix's side while she killed who knew how many others, if not outright doing the killing himself. There could be no truce. He didn't deserve mercy.

Lanthimos struggled but Shane squeezed harder. The pale ghost on the floor began to stir, and Shane leaned forward, forcing Lanthimos against the bed frame with Shane's weight pushing down on him. He felt a snap in the man's neck and then something crunched as his head twisted to the left.

Shane released his arm and Lanthimos slumped over. The house shook as though an earthquake erupted beneath Shane's feet. The pale ghost from the floor turned and swiped clumsily at him. The attack was easily avoided, and Shane forced the spirit down, gripping her head in his hands and applying pressure.

The ghost moaned a confused and distressed sound that cut off with a pop as her head caved in. The darker spirit from the ceiling shrieked and dropped to the floor as Shane was thrust back by the burst of energy.

Half of the ceiling caved in and crushed the bed. Dust rolled out in an ever-expanding cloud and obscured Shane's view of the second ghost. It lashed out with cold hands and Shane caught the wrist of the one he'd already crippled, pulling it closer.

"Filthy!" the ghost hissed.

Shane ignored it, punching it in the face and knocking more of its teeth loose before hitting one of the foul-smelling thing's legs and forcing it to the floor.

Stone buckled beneath his feet, but Shane kept his footing and dropped onto the ghost, breaking its neck with enough force to pull the head free. The explosion pushed him out of the room and into the hallway that connected the front door and the living room.

The house wailed like a mourner at a funeral and Shane struggled toward the sliding door, navigating a floor that rose and fell like the waves of the ocean he could see outside. Timbers fell from the ceiling, and behind him, he heard voices calling his name as other spirits crept from the shadows.

Shane pulled the cobweb-laced curtains from where they were tied next to the broken glass of the sliding door and removed his lighter. He lit the old, dry material and tossed it to the floor in the center of the room. The fire spread quickly, consuming the fabric and spreading to the floorboards and furniture. The house was too old, and the wood too dry and full of cracks. The only chance it had now was if it was strong enough to withstand the fire, if the combined power of the spirits within could overcome the fury of nature.

The wraparound porch crumbled underfoot as Shane left the house, stumbling to the steps and then down onto the wet sand. Inside, the fire had spread to a wall and was slowly rising, consuming the broken old house. It snapped and popped as it spread across the sofa and hutches, licking up the walls to the ceiling and spreading through to other rooms.

Beatrix was long gone. Only one figure was near the house as Shane put distance between himself and the smoking relic. The ghost from the sea he'd met when he arrived watched from the waves but said nothing.

Shane kept moving. Smoke escaped from cracks in the ceiling, and soon, fire was visible on the exterior of the house, first near the living room door but soon enough on the second floor and coming from the roof.

Even though no one went down the road to the house anymore,

people from town would see it soon enough. The smoke and the fire would be visible across the bay, and on the horizon.

Shane headed across the property to the road, back toward where he had left his car, as flames claimed the walls and began to belch huge clouds of black smoke into the sky. Screams came from within, but Shane knew none were from the living. The house had been too damaged during his fight with the boy to stave off the destruction. It died like a living thing, wailing and shaking until the roof collapsed.

The walls had given way by the time Shane reached his car. Flaming debris fell all around the house and the screaming voices faded to nothing. The destruction was much faster than Shane expected. There must have been little more than the power of the ghosts holding the house together, nothing real or from the world of the living. The house should have been destroyed long ago, but the ghosts had held it as long as they could.

Beatrix would not be happy when she found out what happened. The destruction of her brother had pushed her more toward anger than anything else Shane had experienced with her. Previously, she had seemed aloof, even indifferent to serious and dangerous situations. Now, her mood was swinging toward rage.

Shane knew something was broken within Beatrix. Even with the conflicting stories he'd heard from her and Ben, it was clear their childhood had been a nightmare. Their parents would have been powerless against Mr. Shadow and likely didn't know what to do with children who could see and destroy ghosts.

Beatrix had lived according to her moral code, such as it was, for too long. She didn't think like normal people anymore. She was like the dead, all unchecked emotion and dangerous whims that directed her this way or that. She was unhinged and extremely powerful. Dealing with her would not be an easy task, not that he had expected it to be. It just seemed like things were going to be worse now.

Shane drove away from the beach, leaving the flaming rubble of the house in his rearview. He headed through town slowly and casually, so as not to draw attention. He was just another driver going about his business; nothing to do with the haunted house inferno on the beach.

He needed to get back to Nashua. If he could get in touch with James Moran or Xander Ventura, maybe one of them could shed some light on Mr. Shadow.

Once he was out of Rhode Island and back in Massachusetts on the road home, he got in touch with Ventura to loop him in on what he had discovered.

"Her real name is Brandy Jean Talbot," Shane said. "Had a twin brother named Ben who would have died when they were kids. Lived at forty-eight Strand in Tiverton, Rhode Island."

"Hell, what do you need me for if you found all that?" Ventura asked.

"Have to find her now. She's working with someone she called Mr. Shadow."

"That his given name?" the FBI agent asked.

"He's dead. Don't know anything about him except he's been around for a while, and it seems like he's strong. Also, there were more of those Hounds, you find anything there?"

"How many?" Ventura asked.

"Five more. Someone's been brutalizing these people somewhere. There's got to be a lead in there, right?"

"I'm looking," Ventura explained. "Problem is, about fifty thousand people who go missing in America every year are never seen again. We deal with more than four thousand unidentified bodies annually. Hell, six months into the year, and there are already over a thousand missing people in New York alone. This is a needle-in-a-haystack situation."

"Well, how many have their skulls flayed and most of their bones broken?" Shane countered.

"None that I've found. These bodies aren't being dumped for us to find."

"I suppose Beatrix and Shadow might keep them around. Might need them if the ghosts are bound to them. See what you can find on the name. She's going off the rails soon, and it's going to be ugly. She knows where I live; I want to be on the same level."

"I'll get back to you when I can. Where are you now?"

"Heading back to Nashua. Just burned down her beach house, destroyed her brother, and killed her sidekick. Figured I might take a break."

"Please don't tell me about any felonies you're committing," Ventura replied with a groan. Shane ignored him.

"Call me when you know something."

"Will do," Ventura said.

The line went dead, and Shane scrolled through his phone for James Moran's number before clicking the button.

"Shane?" James said by way of greeting. "Are you okay?"

"Mostly," Shane said. "You track down anything new?"

"Nothing useful, I'm afraid. More clients of the Harvesters but nothing that leads to anything we don't know. They go directly to their clients, there's no base of operations or point of contact from which to start a search."

"I've got a name for you, dumb as it sounds. Mr. Shadow."

"Mr. Shadow?" James repeated.

"Old ghost, I think. He's at the top of the food chain, near as I can figure. Beatrix is getting her info from him. Don't know much beyond that, but it's been going by that name for at least a couple of decades."

"A unique moniker, to be sure. I'll see what I can find out. Do you have a description, a haunted item, anything of that nature?"

"Nothing. I mean, I saw the crayon drawings of a child. He's big and black."

"Big and black. That ought to narrow it down," James said. Shane was unable to tell if it was meant to be sarcastic.

"I'm heading home now. Call if you find anything. I've got Ventura looking into her real name, Brandy Jean Talbot. Her base of operations has to be where she's keeping Shadow, and the two of them seem to be running the whole Harvesters operation. Just not sure what the ghost's game is. Or hers, at this point. There's something more than money behind this."

"Yes, most spirits don't find value in a dollar," James agreed. "I'll look into the names and let you know what I find."

Shane hung up and continued home. He was only about an hour away now, but the drive felt much longer. His body ached, his head throbbed, and he felt like he could sleep for a week. But there was no time to rest yet. He was close; he could feel it.

The next time he met Beatrix, he was certain only one of them would walk away.

CHAPTER 24
FAMILIAR GROUND

It was late when Shane arrived in Nashua. He was not sure how long he had been trapped in the house on the beach. Day and night rolled together, formed from illusions created by the house. But it was certainly not as long as Beatrix had hoped it would be.

He pulled onto Berkley Street and drove up toward the house. The place was calm and quiet, the way his property almost always was. He was glad to be home, even if he'd only be there for a short time. With the information he had provided to Ventura and James, Shane felt they would soon come up with something. Beatrix could not hide forever.

His body was a patchwork of pain and bruises. He did not have much left in the tank, but he was not about to quit. He was close and he knew it. He just needed to find a way to end it. Then he could rest and heal. He just needed enough for one last push.

Shane parked the car and turned off the engine. As he left the vehicle, he pulled a pack of cigarettes from his pocket and retrieved one, lighting it as he leaned against the car and looked at the house.

The night was very still, and the smoke rose in a thin, unbroken wisp from the tip of the cigarette. No wind disturbed it, and no sounds broke the night save for the distant din of traffic from somewhere in town.

There was no one in the windows. Shane stared at the house, wondering just how much it was like the one he'd watched burn down on the beach. What would it take for his home to work itself into such a frenzy that it nearly shook itself to the ground? Was it more or less a living, thinking thing than Beatrix's house?

Shane did not understand how this kind of haunted house worked. He had experienced many buildings—houses, hospitals, schools, or otherwise—that were infested with ghosts. None of them worked quite the same way. The buildings rarely took on aspects of the ghosts that haunted them.

It must have something to do with the age of the building. The amount of time it had housed spirits, maybe even bonded with them on some level beyond the understanding of the living.

There had to be a lot of history in the beach house. More than just Beatrix's brother and Mr. Shadow. Beatrix said there were other ghosts in the house. Shane had seen at least four and heard many others. It might have been even more haunted than his home.

None of that mattered now. The house was gone. The fire would have destroyed some of the haunted items, and perhaps the others would survive and just be spirits wandering the beach like the one he'd seen in the ocean.

Even though he had needed to save his own life and escape from the place, there was an odd pang of regret he felt because of what had happened. If not for Beatrix and Mr. Shadow, perhaps those ghosts would have existed peacefully in the house the way Carl and the others did in his. Maybe they deserved that freedom, that peace. But it was taken from them.

Not that they were innocent bystanders, but maybe in their minds, they were just doing what Carl and Eloise and the others would have done to someone if the same sort of thing occurred in the Anderson House. On the other hand, maybe he was just tired and overthinking things.

Shane pinched off the cigarette butt and stood up straight. He walked toward the house in no hurry, crossing the driveway to the front door and reaching for the knob.

He only heard one footstep but couldn't even turn around before he felt the barrel of a gun pressed to the back of his head. The steel was cold, and there was pain as it dug into his flesh right beneath the still-healing injury he'd received from Lanthimos.

"You are so goddamn predictable," Beatrix said. There was amusement in her voice. Shane kept his eyes on the front door, not willing to move with the gun jammed into his head.

"I'd hate to disappoint you," he said.

"Honestly, I debated coming here. I assumed those restraints wouldn't hold you for long, but I questioned whether you'd run home right away or figure something else out first. It came down to a coin toss. And then here you are, right on schedule."

"Isn't that something?" he told her.

"Is Adrian dead?" she asked, her tone more serious now.

"He is," Shane said.

She chuckled and Shane felt the gun shift slightly.

"I figured as much," she said wryly. There wasn't much sorrow or anger in her voice.

"Sounds like you'll be giving him a hell of a eulogy," Shane said.

"Screw him," she replied. "He went behind my back; he got what he deserved."

"He let me go, for what it's worth," Shane said. That made her laugh.

"Of course, he did. Such an asshole. Did you have to convince him?"

"A little bit. He was committed to pretending you two were a team right until he did it."

"Yeah, hell of a team. And look at you, reaping the benefits of our schism. Alive and kicking despite it all."

"Must have a lucky penny in my pocket," Shane said.

"Oh, I don't know that I'd consider myself lucky if I were you," she told him. The gun pushed against the back of his head. "Let's get inside before the neighbors get suspicious."

Shane did as Beatrix asked. He opened the door slowly and stepped across the threshold. She stayed with him, gun in place, and closed the door behind them as they entered the foyer.

The house was dark, which wasn't unexpected. It was also silent, and Shane saw no one around. He had no doubt that the ghosts of the house were aware of Beatrix's presence even before he was, but they had not acted on it. At least not that he had seen.

He didn't know how long Beatrix had been there, but she had not left the beach house much earlier than he had. She had a few hours' head start at most. She could have gone straight to Nashua. If she did, maybe she had already been inside the house. Maybe there was no one left.

As strong as Carl and the others were, he did not think they would be a match for Beatrix if she was committed to taking them out.

"Jesus, this is grim even for you," Beatrix said. "You seriously live in this place full time?"

"My decorator is out of town," Shane replied.

"Your decorator died fifty years before I was born," she said.

From the corner of his eye, he saw her pull open the door on the grandfather clock and run a finger across the surface inside, then close it up again.

"Sorry it's not a burned-down beach house full of corpses," he replied.

There was a pause before she spoke again.

"Burned down," she repeated.

"Like tissue paper. That place was a hell of a tinderbox. Lucky no one worth saving was home."

Beatrix laughed and it sounded almost genuine if a touch manic.

"Of course," she sighed. "You trying to set me off, Solo? Make me lose my cool?"

"Just being honest," he told her.

"Honesty gets people killed, doesn't it? But Mr. Shadow doesn't want you dead just yet. He hasn't even had a face-to-face with you, and he loves those. He loves faces in general. You might have noticed he takes them off the Hounds."

"I did," Shane confirmed.

"He'll probably want to peel that bald dome of yours like a grape when he's done with you, and it's going to be ugly. Don't kid yourself. I've seen it, and even I don't like it. It's still funny, but not ha-ha funny, if you follow me."

"Sounds dramatic," Shane said.

"Very. What do you have to drink in this dump?" she said, pushing him forward with the gun.

"Coffee," he replied. "Water."

"Good God, are you sober?" she said.

He led her from the foyer toward the kitchen in the dark. He paused in the doorway and clicked on the light. The room was empty, as expected. Still no sign of anyone.

"Was for a while. Haven't stopped to pick anything up lately is all."

"Coffee it is. Put on a pot. We can chat for a bit before I bleed you out."

Shane paused, looking at the coffee pot.

"Thought I wasn't going to die yet," he said.

"Who told you that?" she asked, pushing him again.

He filled the machine with water and added a filter and some grounds before turning it on. He still couldn't see her; she stayed close with the gun to the back of his head.

"You did, a minute ago," he answered.

"You don't listen well," she told him.

The gun nudged him again, and she directed him toward a chair, sitting him down. She kept the gun on him as she pulled a chair from the table, giving herself space so that if he reached for the weapon, she'd have time to pull the trigger.

"What I said was that Mr. Shadow doesn't want you dead yet. Has nothing to do with what I'm going to do."

"You're not working together anymore?"

She laughed more bitterly than her previous bouts and smiled at him.

"You're just the worst person, aren't you? Unbearable in every way. There are no more hunts. You know that, right? Because of you. The rest of the team is dead or fled. No one's going to hire us even if I find a new team. The whole thing's screwed because the word is out there. You've got this goddamn... James Moron or whoever he is dragging us through the mud for anyone who will listen. I got the FBI asking questions, and I know that's you, too. I lost a half-dozen trophies in, what, two days? All thanks to you. Goddamn."

She aimed the gun between his eyes, her hand steady as a rock. She was barely even blinking.

"Happy to have made a difference," Shane told her.

Behind him, the coffee maker hissed and sputtered as the pot filled. The smell of coffee filled the room.

"Oh, I know you are, Solo. I know you've got a bag of a thousand and one hilarious quips and barbs, and we can trade one-liners until the sun comes up and I make you cook us some delicious hash browns and over-easy eggs like an old married couple."

"I don't have hash browns," Shane said.

Her arm moved, barely at all, and the gun fired. The bullet grazed the side of Shane's head and embedded itself in the kitchen wall. He felt the burn across the side of his skull like a branding iron had just kissed his flesh, and then it faded into a throbbing sting. The gun was back, aimed dead-center in his face before he could blink.

"Don't ruin my good mood, Solo. If I start feeling like you're not benefitting from our chat, I'll vacate your brains across that Walmart coffee pot back there."

"Got it at Home Depot," he said by way of a correction.

He was pressing his luck a lot, and he knew it, but there had to be a reason she hadn't killed him yet if that was her ultimate goal.

Beatrix leaned in a little closer, still too far for him to make a play for the gun without being shot. Her reflexes were keen, and her aim was impeccable. He'd never make it in time.

"You ever eaten human flesh, Solo?" she asked.

"What?"

The question caught him off-guard.

"Have you. Ever eaten. Human flesh?"

"Can't say that I have."

"I can," she told him. "After I left home. After Shadow took me in. He's not the nurturing type, you understand. No matter how special and unique he said I was. Not a top-shelf father figure. Doesn't go grocery shopping for school lunches; I'll tell you that. If I wanted to live, I had to make do. And even when I didn't want to live, and you'd better believe there were a lot of times when I didn't—"

She raised her empty hand and held it up, wrist out, for Shane to see the patchwork of scars that covered the surface. The wounds overlapped, made from different tools at different times.

"—I was forced to stay alive, so I did what I had to do. I always do. For better or worse, I do whatever I need to do to live. Do you understand what that means, Solo?"

He did not. But the tone of Beatrix's voice had grown more dire and insistent, and she was clenching her jaw and almost shaking by the end of it.

"Why are you telling me this?" Shane asked.

"I am telling you this so that when you die, you know who killed you. You don't know me, Solo. Adrian didn't know me. Ben didn't know me. Mr. Shadow only thinks he knows me because 'he raised me', but no one outside of my skull and soul knows me. Do you want to know who is going to take your life tonight?"

Shane stared at her for a long moment. Her jaw trembled. Her free hand shook, and her eyes were red as tears welled in them. But her gun hand was rocksteady. It never wavered once.

"I do," he answered.

CHAPTER 25
TO TAKE A LIFE

The gurgling of the coffee pot stopped. Shane remained seated, watching the woman with the gun trained on his face. She laughed and then covered her mouth with her free hand before wiping the tears from her eyes.

"Do you know who you are?" she asked, shaking her head.

"I have a good idea."

She laughed again, a derisive scoff.

"Sure, you do. Tough guy from the military. 'This is my rifle, this is my gun,' all that war movie crap. Bet you killed civilians. Popped 'em like balloons, didn't you? Then you come here and act like I'm a monster because I'm not doing it in a foreign land."

"Thought you knew everything about me," he said.

"I know enough. And you knew nothing about me when you came into my world, my life, and you went on to ruin every goddamn thing I had. What gave you the right?"

"You were murdering people. You let dangerous ghosts loose for sport."

"So?" she said.

"So? When a dog gets rabies, you put it down. It's the smart thing to do."

"Well, aren't we offensive?" She laughed then, a quick burst. It was cheery and ecstatic, and she covered her mouth again as she grinned behind it. Her mood had swung dramatically in seconds.

Shane feared she was losing her grip a bit, maybe having a manic episode that was focused on a revenge fantasy about him. It would be hard to rationalize anything with her if that was ever a possibility.

"You shouldn't have gone after Ben," she said, shaking her head. "He was good. He was a good boy. A good brother."

"He was dead," Shane said. "He was full of rage against you and Shadow. You know that, don't you?"

"He loved me," she replied. "And I loved him! We were twins. We were the same."

"Didn't sound like he felt the same."

"I know the truth. That's what matters. I had someone who loved me, and someone I loved. What do you have?"

Shane shrugged. He was plotting a way to get the gun from her, but she was not offering any openings.

"What *do* you have?" she repeated, her eyes narrowing. "Who lives here with you?"

"No one," Shane said.

When he told her he thought she knew everything about him, he had meant it. He assumed she had gathered some intelligence. But the question seemed genuine.

She got to her feet then, suspicion plain on her face.

"Hell of a big house for a lone man to call home," she said.

She circled wide around the table, keeping her distance, with the gun still trained on him. Beatrix began opening drawers and cupboards, looking through his cups and plates and silverware.

"Jesus, four spoons, four forks. Three mugs. Who buys three mugs?" she said.

"The mugs were a set," Shane replied. "Broke one when a ghost attacked me."

Beatrix scoffed, pushing things aside to look through his canned goods.

"Don't do a lot of entertaining," he pointed out.

"I imagine anyone who came to one of your parties would want to kill themselves," she said.

She had not received any background on him. If Mr. Shadow or someone associated with the Harvesters had gotten his address for her, all they had found was where he lived. They knew nothing else. Which meant she didn't know about the ghosts, either.

"Canned peas, huh? You keep getting worse," she said, closing the cupboard. She was behind him now, and he didn't bother to turn his head. She was rifling through another cupboard; he could hear things moving. She might not have had the gun on him anymore, but he didn't risk looking.

A moment later, she came around his side with a cup of coffee in her hand. She set the cup on the table and then sat down again.

"Mind if I get one?" he asked.

"Yes," she said, taking a sip of hers while keeping her eyes locked on him. She made a face and set the cup on the table. "Tastes like burned wood chips."

"Cheapest stuff Walmart has," he told her.

"I bet it is," she said, still grimacing. "You live alone. Divorced?"

"No," he said.

"Can't imagine a woman putting up with you. Was this your parents' house?"

"It was," he said.

Beatrix laughed, her grin spreading across her face.

"Okay, that makes sense. Real *Psycho* vibe here. Mom's skeleton isn't up in the bedroom, is it?"

"Is this how you plan to kill me? Just making me listen to your middle school takes on my life and emotional breakdowns about your Greek tragedy of a childhood? Let me put my head in the oven and end it faster."

She laughed again, musical and full of joy, and then took another sip of coffee that made her grimace once more.

"God, you wish. It's going to last. I got nowhere to be, Solo. This is going to go on for days."

Beatrix looked as though she was ready to continue, but the sound of a door closing deeper in the house gave her pause. Her eyes widened, if only just, and Shane watched her arm extend a little bit as her muscles stiffened.

"Now what do we think that was?" she asked softly.

"Maybe the wind," he replied.

"Who else is here, Solo? I'll kill them first if I have to go looking. I'll make it ugly."

"It's an old house," Shane said. "It makes noises."

"Up," she said, gesturing with the gun.

Shane did as instructed and got to his feet. Beatrix gestured toward the door and kept her distance, the gun aimed and ready, and fell in line behind him.

"Let's go exploring. Lead the way," she said.

Shane started walking down the hall and Beatrix kept pace. He turned lights on as he went, exposing empty hallways and empty rooms. She made him stop and enter so she could look around each room they passed.

There were no signs of life in any of the first handful of rooms. She chose which direction they went, and he offered no argument or assistance in helping her navigate the house.

"What's upstairs?" she asked as they reached the staircase.

"What's usually on the second floor of a house?" he replied.

The barrel of the gun pushed against the back of his head.

"Not the time to get smart," she told him.

They made their way up the stairs, each step creaking ominously as they went. The house was not moving on its own, nor making noise on its own, but the floor was creating new, louder sounds than it had ever made in Shane's experience.

The library was waiting on the second floor, its door open immediately to the left of the staircase. This was not the usual location of the library, but Shane said nothing about it. The lights were already on.

Beatrix pushed Shane aside first and stayed in the doorway to look around.

"Didn't see any lights on when I was outside," she pointed out.

"Maybe you checked the wrong windows," Shane said.

"Maybe I'll splatter your brains across *The Great Gatsby*," she countered.

Shane had not moved from where she had forced him to go. He could see that the bookcase covering the oubliette had been moved, the secret hiding place that held Carl's remains exposed. Mr. Anderson had dropped Carl in there to die years earlier and, aside from Shane, almost no one in the world knew of its existence. He had never left it open.

"What is that, a secret tunnel?" Beatrix asked, taking note of the hole in the stone floor.

"See for yourself," Shane suggested.

"Oh, could I?"

She forced Shane forward. With her free hand, she grabbed the back of Shane's collar and twisted it. She pushed him until he was leaning over the entrance.

"Seen one of these before," she pointed out. "You drop someone down there, they don't come out, huh?"

The barrel of the gun was right behind Shane's ear. He caught a flicker of movement from the corner of his eye but couldn't guess what ghost it was. Whoever it was, Beatrix saw as well and quickly pulled him away from the oubliette.

"Who's in here?" she said very quietly.

"I don't know," he answered honestly.

She backed away another step, dragging Shane with her. She was moving cautiously, keeping her head on a swivel, and watching the room as she directed Shane back to the door.

"I'm not saying I'm immune to traps, but you need to do better than this."

She wasn't talking to Shane, she was talking to whoever else was there, even if she wasn't sure who or what it was.

"This your buddy Moron?" she asked. "Maybe your FBI friend? You don't seem the type to carry more than two friends at a time, tops."

Shane didn't bother to answer. They were back in the hallway, and she forced him down the hall to check out a bedroom and a bathroom.

Another door closed, this one much more powerfully. The sound came from the first floor, and Shane felt the vibration through his feet.

"Sounds like bait to me. You?" she whispered to Shane.

"Sounds like a door," he said.

"Yeah... what do you think would happen if I just blasted your kneecaps and made you crawl downstairs to meet your friend?"

"Personally, I'm against it," he told her.

She nudged him to the stairs, and they headed back down. Shane saw nothing and heard nothing on the way. Whatever the ghosts had planned, they were keeping it well under wraps.

Before he left, Shane had made it clear that Beatrix was a danger. He made sure that all the ghosts in the house knew that she had the same abilities he had and had explained what she did as a Harvester. He told them about Cassius and the Hounds.

The warnings had been to ensure that they approached her with caution if she appeared. More specifically, so that they wouldn't approach her at all. But he knew them well enough to expect they would never hide from her. It was unlike Carl, Eloise, or even the Davis sisters to stand back and watch.

They would have been more direct with another intruder. The house itself would have been more direct. The subtlety of whatever was happening surprised him. Beatrix could only be walked on a leash so far, though. She would tire of the game soon, then her unpredictability would take over.

The only upside so far seemed to be that she was unaware that Shane's house was haunted. It seemed inconceivable at first that she wouldn't have assumed it, but another thought occurred to Shane.

Beatrix had made a point of saying that Mr. Shadow told her how special she was. That was part of the reason he took her in, because of who she was and what she could do. Without her brother, she must have felt unique in the world. She was special. She was the only person like her, seeing and hurting ghosts the way she did.

Even when confronted with Shane, with the knowledge she was not unique, she had not considered what that meant. She couldn't conceive of Shane living in a haunted house because, in her world, no one chose to live in a haunted house. Only her. Only the unique, singular person she was. So, the noises in the house had to be James, or Ventura, or someone else. Someone alive.

That was Beatrix's blind spot. Shane just needed to find a way to exploit it without tipping his hand.

Shane turned his head, a quick twitch, to glance toward the butler's pantry. He righted his head immediately, eyes front and going where he was told to go. The gun pressed harder against his skull.

"What was that?" she asked, closer to him than he thought she was. He could feel her breath in his ear.

"What was what?"

"What were you looking for down that hall?"

She pushed his head left, and forced him to look down at the dark hallway in which end the door to the butler's pantry waited.

"Just a hallway. Thought you might want to go that way," he replied.

"Did you?"

She grabbed the back of his collar again, turning him physically this time.

"Yeah, I do want to go that way. Let's go see what's waiting for us."

Shane did as directed. The first door on his left was just a storage closet. It usually was, anyway. But as he pulled it open, the hinges making far more noise than they ever had, he and Beatrix were greeted by the butler's pantry.

CHAPTER 26
DON'T GO INTO THE DARK

"Swanky stuff, Solo. Did you ever have an actual butler?" Beatrix asked, recognizing the room for what it was.

"No," he said.

She forced him inside.

"So, what, were you the scullery maid in here? Polishing the silver for Mommy and Daddy when they had their rich friends over?"

"It's just a room to store stuff," he told her.

"Such as?"

"China. Tea pots. Tablecloths," he said.

The floor groaned under his feet. The trapdoor to the cellar had moved. He stood on the wooden panel, and it dipped as though threatening to buckle under his weight. Beatrix took a step back.

"How many tablecloths you got down there?" she asked.

"Jars down there, mostly. Old pickled vegetables. Came with the house. I wouldn't recommend eating any of it."

A quiet thump from the cellar vibrated the floor. Beatrix pulled Shane backward off the trapdoor.

"Open it," she ordered.

"There's nothing you want to see down there, I promise."

"You promise?" She laughed and kicked the back of his right knee. He fell to the floor, and the gun clicked above his head.

"Open it," she said again.

Shane did as he was told, lifting the trapdoor, and exposing the deep, cold darkness of what waited below. There were no sounds now, and the cellar smelled like old, forgotten things. The air was cold and stale, but nothing moved. Not yet.

Beatrix's boot hit the back of his head, and he fell forward, hitting the ladder on the way down before the packed earth floor below. He lay there, feeling a sharp pain in his side and the back of his head as she followed him down, taking the steps slowly with the gun on him the entire time.

"Where's the light?" she asked.

"There isn't one," he answered, still on his back on the ground.

She got off the ladder and stood next to him in the dim square of light from the pantry.

"Lights or I put a bullet in your leg," she said.

"There are no lights down here. It's meant to be dark," he explained.

Hinges creaked and the light above them went out. The trapdoor slammed shut and Beatrix swore.

Shane rolled to one side, and the gun fired. He heard the bullet hit the ground where he had just been lying. In the quick flare of the muzzle, shadows darted along the walls. The Dark Ones rushed forth, whispering terrible things as they did so, surrounding the two living people.

"Unexpected," one of the Dark Ones whispered.

"Not unwelcome," another added.

"Jesus, Solo. You keep a basement full of ghosts?" Beatrix said with a laugh.

A light came on and Shane looked back, seeing her there with the gun in one hand and her cell phone flashlight in the other.

The twisted forms of the Dark Ones scuttled out of the light's beam when it crossed their paths, retreating and regrouping each time.

"You're going to want to keep them in hand or you're a dead man," she recommended. The gun was still aimed at where he sat on the dirt floor.

"Dead man," one of the Dark Ones echoed.

"Oh yes. Do it."

176

"Do it! Bleed him dry!"

Her words excited the dark spirits, and she laughed even harder at their chorus of threats and suggestions.

"Even your ghosts hate you," she said delightedly.

"They're not mine," Shane said. "They came with the house."

One of the Dark Ones slithered up from the shadows behind Beatrix and wrapped an arm around her throat.

"A new one to enjoy," it hissed in her ear.

Beatrix dropped her phone and the gun. The light pointed up, allowing Shane to see what was happening as she pulled the Dark One's arm away from her, catching it by surprise as it did not expect to confront someone else who could fight back.

She was as swift and brutal as Shane expected her to be. With one arm, she held the Dark One tight against her body, and with the other, she hooked her fingers into its mouth and peeled back its head like an orange.

The decapitation was in such a fluid motion that she was able to fling the body away as it came apart and exploded. The blast knocked some of the other spirits back and hit Shane with a firm but tolerable push.

Some of the others shrieked, and two came at her simultaneously. Another took the opportunity to go for Shane as he got to his feet.

Beatrix wrestled with one of her attackers, cursing the ghosts and Shane. Shane was forced to peel his own Dark One off his back, taking it down to the ground again and hammering on the dark, formless face of the shadowy thing with his fist.

Another blast came after Beatrix destroyed the second Dark One. The third was from Shane taking out his.

Beatrix screamed, not in pain but in rage. She threw the second Dark One at Shane like a bag of trash and dove for her gun. Eloise caught her wrist before she could grasp it, twisting the woman's arm back.

"That's not yours anymore," the girl said.

Beatrix's expression was primal hatred. She swung her free hand, lining up a punch to take Eloise in the face, when her other wrist was caught by one of the Davis sisters.

Carl lifted Beatrix by a handful of her hair, pulling her away from the gun. The woman struggled, kicking out at whichever of the sisters had her wrist, but another took her place, with the third sister moving in close and whispering something in Beatrix's ear.

She screamed again and then Eloise snapped her wrist. Carl dragged her to the ground, and the three sisters swarmed her, moving less like humans and more like pack animals. Their hands were almost synchronized, up and down movements as Beatrix cursed and thrashed and tried to fight her way free.

Scraps of bloody clothing were tossed across the cellar. Beatrix's screams changed in pitch and volume. What had once been hatred and anger became overwhelmed by pain.

It only lasted seconds. Shane heard a wet, snapping sound, and Beatrix's voice was cut off. Carl stood up as the sisters and Eloise continued their assault. He made eye contact with Shane.

"That's enough," Shane said, approaching the body.

"We have to make sure she's dead," Daphne said.

"Wouldn't want a mistake," Dora added.

"Pays to be thorough," Daisy finished.

"It's enough," he said again.

The sisters backed away reluctantly, leaving only Eloise with the woman's body. She looked up at Shane and said nothing. Her hands were on Beatrix's head, but the woman's body had been almost gutted. The sisters had torn out her insides. Marks around her throat showed that someone had choked her as well.

Eloise snapped Beatrix's neck. When she was done, she repositioned the head so the woman was looking up. She stared at the body for a moment and then closed Beatrix's eyes before she stood.

In the background, the remaining Dark Ones were gathering once more, whispering and threatening. They had lost three of their number and had retreated but were emboldening themselves once again.

"What will we do with the body?" Carl asked.

Shane did not have to answer. He knew the house would take care of it. It always did.

"Leave it," one of the Dark Ones whispered.

"Leave it for us!"

"Leave it," Shane said with a shrug.

He climbed the steps out of the cellar and returned to the main floor. Once the trap door was closed again, he could hear the Dark Ones below, reveling in what had happened. That three of them having been destroyed seemed to mean nothing; they were just excited by the chaos and death.

Shane returned to the kitchen. The coffee was still hot, and he poured himself a cup. He sat at the table and the ghosts of the house joined him. Herbert and Thaddeus appeared as well, though they had stayed out of the fight.

"We saw her here before you arrived, but she did not enter, so we thought it best to not reveal ourselves," Carl explained. "I did not anticipate her bringing you in at gunpoint."

"She was creative like that," Shane said. "It's fine. You came through."

"I liked her insides," Daphne said then giggled.

"She didn't deserve them," Dora added.

"She was unwelcome," Daisy said.

"What about the others?" Herbert asked. "There are more Harvesters, aren't there?"

"Not anymore," Shane said.

That wasn't entirely true. If there was more of the group, they were likely gone, as Beatrix has said. But there was still the matter of Mr. Shadow.

"Then it's over?" Eloise asked.

She was looking at Shane with a very serious expression. He took a sip of coffee and then set the cup down.

"I don't know," he answered honestly.

Without Beatrix as his envoy to the world, Mr. Shadow would certainly be crippled. But the ghost had some kind of mission. There had to be a reason behind why he did what he did. It seemed like he had dedicated years to building up to something.

Unless Agent Ventura and James discovered new information, there were still a lot of missing people. A lot of people had been murdered for the sake of the ghosts that Beatrix called Hounds.

Shane didn't think that would have been a one-man operation. These people had to be held somewhere. They were being tortured but they were also being kept alive. They were being molded into monsters, and that required time and privacy.

Beatrix was working on the back end of things. She was making money. Someone else had to be helping Mr. Shadow with his monstrous zoo. Someone else was still out there somewhere, using the money she'd been earning.

And they wanted something more.

EPILOGUE

The sky was overcast. The threat of rain had loomed for more than a day. The man knew it would come soon enough. He had always enjoyed the rain. A powerful storm that showed the fury of nature. It gave him pleasure.

Wind, rain, and lightning were destructive. They could destroy anything man created. But there was no intention behind it. The rain didn't fall maliciously; the wind didn't blow things over because it hated them. They just happened. They couldn't even be considered indifferent; they had no emotions. That was something glorious. That was something to be respected as much as it was to be feared.

He drove slowly along rural roads. Great, green forest grew all around him. The land was vibrant and full of life. Anything full of life was equally full of death. One couldn't exist without the other, and so he respected each in turn. He revered them and was enamored by the mysteries of each.

The man had spent years studying how life and death worked. Few people could teach the mysteries he had unlocked on his own. Few people even understood they existed, and fewer still had the nerve to explore what that meant.

He was forced to take up the mantle of master and student in one. He learned as he went, he observed what he could, and he tested theories as he gained a clearer understanding. There had been many failures, but there had been successes. He doubted there were many people in the world who could do half of what he could.

The old truck rumbled along the road until he found his turnoff. It was marked by a red flag tied to the branch of a tree next to an unpaved path into the woods. It was not inviting to strangers. It was not the sort of place most people would go to unless they had reason to. Those who took the path uninvited would find nothing hospitable at the end of the road.

The path through the woods was not smooth, and the truck bounced and jostled. The old man behind the wheel found it uncomfortable, but many things were uncomfortable these days. He had lived a long life, and though he was far from finished with it, it seemed like it was getting closer to being finished with him.

He woke up with aches and pains that he went to sleep to get rid of. His joints and his muscles screamed when he overexerted himself. He was now at the point that he could feel the storms coming. Barometric pressure worked on his knees as much as it worked on the air.

Still, his hands were steady enough when there was work to be done. His eyesight was keen and clear. He could do the precision work he needed to do. He could still create perfection. The moment that was no longer the case, he would quit, and that would be it.

He had worked for many clients over the years. Some called themselves his bosses, or his masters, or anything that implied that they had power, and he was a servant. He didn't mind. Labels meant nothing to him.

What mattered was the work he did. He chose opportunities that allowed him to expand and grow. He would never take a similar job twice because there was nothing to be learned. Money was pointless. He didn't do the work to get paid. Not that he didn't charge great sums, but that was for show and to weed out the unserious.

For the experience, he allowed the people he worked with to call him whatever they wanted and make whatever lofty demands and proclamations they felt necessary. He could not have cared less about the motivations, so long as he could do what he wanted.

When he started, he called himself a necromancer. Sometimes, they called him simpler things, like a medium. Even a spiritualist. They reduced him to things as simple as a psychic in some circles. What did it matter? It was not his place to police the thoughts and opinions of others.

Few clients had a greater worldview and a greater understanding. Those were the ones he appreciated the most. The ones who saw the potential and had ideas that even he had not considered. That was why he was heading to the long-forgotten estate, deep in the woods of Vermont. This was the greatest job he had ever done.

The forest gave way, and he was soon greeted by the large, run-down estate. No one had taken care of the land in some time, not that it needed it. Guests did not come here unless they had a very specific reason.

He stopped the truck at the front door and got out. The air was so clean there, and different from the city in so many ways. Sometimes, he thought he might like to live in a place like that, far away from everyone and everything. Maybe if he ever retired. Maybe if he lived that long.

No one had told him when the mansion was built or who owned it, not that he had ever asked. It wasn't a relevant detail to the work he did, but it didn't mean he wasn't curious. Someone had once put a lot of care into that house. It was probably the pride and joy of its owner once upon a time. But that was a long time ago.

The roof sagged now. Many of the windows were clouded with years of grime. There were cracks in the stone, and places where the wood warped and paint peeled away. Like the man himself, the house was old and falling apart a little bit. It would collapse one day, and eventually, the forest would reclaim it. Life and death couldn't be avoided.

The door opened easily. It had not been locked in many years. The inside of the house fared better than the exterior, but not much. It was very dusty, and cobwebs had built up in the corners. It smelled old and musty, the way unused things did. The sagging roof would eventually give way, the rain and snow would get into the house, and it would start to smell of mold and rot. But it hadn't yet.

He made his way past a dozen empty rooms to the stairs and headed down into the basement. The basement was dark, but he didn't need a light to show him the way. He had traveled the path enough times before, and no surprises waited for him.

A faint and muffled scream came to his ears through the stone walls as he passed a padlocked room. He paid it no mind. The other rooms along the hall were sealed with the same locks. He could hear weeping from some and screams in others, but many were silent. They all went silent eventually.

He continued deeper into the vast basement. None of the locked chambers had what he was searching for. Instead, he found a room at the end of a long corridor, sealed behind a heavy wooden door. There was no lock on this one, nor had there ever been.

The door pushed open easily despite its size. There was a faint, yellow light, as though from a candle even though no flame burned. It came from nothing, a quirk of the powers of those who no longer lived. He had studied it before. Corpse lights, he called them. They burned because the dead willed them to burn.

The corpse lights in the room were dim, as they always were, and existed solely for his benefit. He could see the shape on the far wall, sitting cross-legged in a shadow that seemed to exist in defiance of those yellow spots of illumination.

The figure was taller than any man should be, even when seated. He was broad of shoulder and long of limb. Everything was exaggerated just enough that it hit the eye wrong. Too tall, legs too long, fingers too spindly. It bordered on caricature but didn't quite reach that point. The result was not something alien and clearly wrong, but something familiar yet uncanny. Something that appeared wrong but in a way that was hard to quantify without spending time studying him and what was incorrect. The old man had spent the time doing that.

He was not alone in the darkness. Two figures waited on either side, crouched on haunches like animals, though anatomically, they were very nearly human. They had started as humans, after all. Now they were more.

Their broken limbs and flayed faces were hallmarks of the man's artistry; of the creations his client had ordered. He called them Hounds. They were why he had come.

"I'm afraid the Hounds have perished," the man said. "There are none left in the field."

The dark shape did not respond. The man had not expected him to.

"Mr. Lanthimos took possession of the final brood. He was acting on his own, as I understand it. He sought to defy Beatrix, and you, I suppose. He wanted to capture this Shane Ryan on his own."

There was a rumble in the shadows, an acknowledgment of what was said.

"The house in Rhode Island is no more. It has burned down," the man continued. "I can't say with certainty if Mr. Ryan, Mr. Lanthimos, or Beatrix was responsible. All were present."

The corpse lights extinguished, and the man stood in pitch black. It was as much of an emotional response as he had ever gotten from Mr. Shadow. The house was important to the spirit, the man knew.

"The boy."

The words came from the dark, from all of it all at once. It was like being in Mr. Shadow's mind as he thought the words rather than hearing them spoken. The man felt them in his bones.

"Unclear," the man replied. "I assume gone? But in my experience, it is never wise to make assumptions in circumstances like these. All I can confirm is that if he still exists, I do not know where he is."

There was shuffling in the darkness, and the man waited for it to stop.

"And," he added, "I do not know what has become of Beatrix."

The woman could have been dead. She could have joined her brother in the fire and been killed. But, knowing her, she was just as likely to have made a miraculous escape and vanished into the night. The man knew her more by reputation than anything else, but in their few interactions, he had determined that she was not someone to be underestimated despite her outward demeanor. Mr. Shadow did not place his trust in her lightly.

"Breed me a new army," Mr. Shadow said.

The voice cut through the man's flesh, and he felt it in his guts. There was power in the voices of the dead, something the man had studied like he had studied the corpse lights. It was difficult, however, and few volunteered to speak for the sake of research. From his experiences, the man knew that when the dead spoke, the living were inclined to flee. He could feel the urge inside him even though his rational mind quelled it.

"How many?" the man asked.

"As many as you can."

Some in the cells were ready, but he would have to work harder to produce enough. Making a Hound was not easy. The time and patience required could not be rushed, and Mr. Shadow knew it. And he was not asking for a rush job; he was asking for a thorough one.

They would need more breeders. The best breeders were already partially broken. People who had lost their way but had not sunk fully into despair. The man had learned this early when he had used drug addicts and the homeless. He had assumed that they would be ideal subjects. Again, assumptions were not always correct.

Instead, he needed someone who was almost broken but still held hope. Those who believed that tomorrow was a new day, that there was light at the end of the tunnel. Those made the best candidates. He would break them again and again and again. Not just mentally but physically. He would mold them into monsters because that was what he did. He was the Houndmaster, and he created nightmares no one else had imagined.

"I'll start work right away," the Houndmaster said.

The task was a daunting one. For every person the Harvesters brought in and every cell they filled, only a fraction would make it to become a Hound. Most would die and not return. Some would come back wrong, ineffectual, or unfinished. Sometimes, they went through one or two dozen just to get one success.

He would have to join the hunt this time. The Harvesters were not as skilled at picking subjects. He would ensure it was done correctly.

"Should we look for Beatrix?" the Houndmaster asked, a last-minute thought before leaving the room to start his work.

"No," Mr. Shadow answered. "We don't need her anymore. I've found who I've been looking for."

The Houndmaster paused. Mr. Shadow rarely explained anything outside the scope of his work. He was not even aware that Mr. Shadow was looking for someone explicitly.

"Shane Ryan?" he inquired, letting curiosity get the best of him.

"No," Mr. Shadow said again. "James Moran."

Check out these best-selling series from our talented authors:

GHOST STORIES

RON RIPLEY
BERKLEY STREET SERIES
MOVING IN SERIES
HAUNTED COLLECTION SERIES
DEATH HUNTER SERIES

IAN FORTEY
JIGSAW OF SOULS SERIES
CULT OF THE ENDLESS NIGHT SERIES

SUPERNATURAL SUSPENSE

A. I. NASSER
SLAUGHTER SERIES
SIN SERIES

DAVID LONGHORN
NIGHTMARE SERIES
ASYLUM SERIES

SARA CLANCY
THE BELL WITCH SERIES
BANSHEE SERIES

For a complete list of our new releases and best-selling horror books, visit
ScareStreet.com or scan the QR code below!

www.ingramcontent.com/pod-product-compliance
Lightning Source LLC
Chambersburg PA
CBHW050345030726
47503CB00008B/2629